An Anthology of
Spanish American Modernismo

Texts and Translations

The Texts and Translations series was founded in 1991 to provide students and teachers with important texts not readily available or not available at an affordable price and in high-quality translations. The books in the series are intended for students in upper-level undergraduate and graduate courses in national literatures in languages other than English, comparative literature, ethnic studies, area studies, translation studies, women's studies, and gender studies. The Texts and Translations series is overseen by an editorial board composed of specialists in several national literatures and in translation studies.

For a complete listing of titles, see the last pages of this book.

An Anthology of Spanish American Modernismo

In English Translation, with Spanish Text

Edited by
Kelly Washbourne

Translated by
Kelly Washbourne
with Sergio Waisman

The Modern Language Association of America
New York 2007

Library of Congress Cataloging-in-Publication Data

An anthology of Spanish American modernismo : in English translation, with Spanish text / edited by Kelly Washbourne ; translated by Kelly Washbourne ; with Sergio Waisman.
p. cm.
Includes bibliographical references and index.
ISBN: 978-0-87352-939-6 (pbk. : alk. paper)
1. Spanish American poetry—19th century—Translations into English. 2. Spanish American poetry—19th century. 3. Modernism (Literature)—Latin America. I. Washbourne, Kelly. II. Waisman, Sergio Gabriel.
PQ7087.E5A48 2007
861'.6408112—dc22 2007022812

ISSN 1079-252x
ISSN 1079-2538

Cover illustration: *Dead Poet Borne by a Centaur*, by Gustave Moreau. Watercolor. Musée Gustave Moreau, Paris.
Photo credit: Réunion des Musées Nationaux / Art Resource, NY

Printed on recycled paper

Published by The Modern Language Association of America
26 Broadway, New York, New York 10004-1789
www.mla.org

For Camelly and my mother
—KW

For Maureen and Emma
—SW

Contents

Introduction xi
Suggestions for Further Reading xxxix
Primary Texts xli
Note on the Translations xliii

José Martí (Cuba; 1853–95)

Sueño despierto / I Dream Awake 5
Musa traviesa / Naughty Muse 7
Amor de ciudad grande / Love in the City 23
Si ves un monte de espumas . . . / If you see a mountain of ocean spray . . . 29
Dos patrias / Two Countries 31
Siempre que hundo la mente / Whenever I Plunge My Mind 33
Contra el verso retórico . . . / Against Rhetorical Poetry . . . 35

Salvador Díaz Mirón (Mexico; 1853–1928)

Cleopatra / Cleopatra 41
Música fúnebre / Funeral Music 45

Manuel Gutiérrez Nájera (Mexico; 1859–95)

To Be / To Be 49
Para entonces / When My Time Comes 53
Mis enlutadas / My Ladies in Mourning 55

Julián del Casal (Cuba; 1863–93)

Mis amores: Soneto Pompadour / My Loves: Pompadour Sonnet 65
Flores de éter / Flowers of Ether 67
Neurosis / Neurosis 75
En el campo / In the Country 79

José Asunción Silva (Colombia; 1865–96)

Nocturno III / Nocturne III 85
Ars / Ars Poetica 91
Vejeces / Things Past 93
El mal del siglo / *Mal du Siècle* 97
Melancolía / Melancholia 99

Rubén Darío (Nicaragua; 1867–1916)

El cisne / The Swan 103
El reino interior / The Kingdom Within 105
Yo persigo una forma . . . / I Seek a Form . . . 113
La página blanca / The Blank Page 115
A Roosevelt / To Roosevelt 119
¡Torres de Dios! ¡Poetas! . . . / Towers of God! Poets! . . . 125
¡Carne, celeste carne de la mujer . . . ! / Flesh, Heavenly Flesh of Woman . . . ! 127
En las constelaciones / In the Constellations 131

Ricardo Jaimes Freyre (Bolivia; 1868–1933)

Æternum vale / Æternum vale ("Farewell Forever") 135
El canto del mal / The Song of Evil 139
Las voces tristes / The Doleful Cries 141
Lo fugaz / Ephemera 143

Amado Nervo (Mexico; 1870–1919)

Edelweiss / Edelweiss 147
Al cruzar los caminos / At the Crossroads 151

José Juan Tablada (Mexico; 1871–1945)

Misa negra / Black Mass 155
Quinta Avenida / Fifth Avenue 159
Haikai (selectos) / Selected Haiku 161

Enrique González Martínez (Mexico; 1871–1952)

Tuércele el cuello al cisne . . . / Wring the Neck of the Swan . . . 165
Busca en todas las cosas / Search Out in All Things 167

Guillermo Valencia (Colombia; 1873–1943)

Cigüeñas blancas (fragmentos) / White Storks (excerpts) 173
Anarkos (fragmento) / Anarchos (excerpt) 183

José María Eguren (Peru; 1874–1942)

Marcha fúnebre de una Marionnette / Funeral March of a Marionette 193
Los reyes rojos / The Red Kings 197
La dama i / Lady i 199
Peregrín cazador de figuras / Peregrine the Image Hunter 201

Leopoldo Lugones (Argentina; 1874–1938)

A Histeria / To Hysteria 205
Delectación morosa / Sullen Delights 209
Divagación lunar / Lunar Digressions 211
La blanca soledad / White Solitude 219
Historia de mi muerte / Story of My Death 223

Julio Herrera y Reissig (Uruguay; 1875–1910)

La vuelta de los campos / Return from the Fields 227
Tertulia lunática (fragmento) / Lunatic Gathering (excerpt) 229
Decoración heráldica / Heraldic Decoration 235
Desolación absurda (fragmento) / Absurd Desolation (excerpt) 237
Neurastenia / Neurasthenia 251

María Eugenia Vaz Ferreira (Uruguay; 1875–1924)

Rendición / Surrender 255
Yo sola / I Alone 257
Los desterrados / The Exiles 259

José Santos Chocano (Peru; 1875–1934)

Las orquídeas / Orchids 267
Oda salvaje (fragmentos) / Wild Ode (excerpts) 269

Juana Borrero (Cuba; 1877–96)

Apolo / Apollo 283
Las hijas de Ran / The Daughters of Ran 285
Íntima / Intimate 287

Delmira Agustini (Uruguay; 1886–1914)

El intruso / The Intruder 291
Las alas / The Wings 293
Lo inefable / The Ineffable 297
Nocturno / Nocturnal 299
El cisne / The Swan 303
Nocturno / Nocturne 309

Works Cited in the Headnotes and Footnotes 311

INTRODUCTION

Tuércele el cuello al cisne de engañoso plumaje . . .

—Enrique Gonález Martínez

Wring the neck of the swan with his feathers false . . .

Why "unwring the swan's neck" after more than a century's strangling of modernismo's emblematic bird? Modernismo calls for a reexamination precisely now that critical frameworks—cultural studies, inter-American studies, gender theory, postcolonial studies, literary historiography—are revealing new approaches to reading the past. The new translations of this volume, many of them first translations, can help move this literary moment from the museum, as modernismo has outlived its fashionable dismissal as a rearguard group of solipsists trapped inside language (a sadly ironic appraisal, since they began in revolution). Such dismissal is the provenance of the rivaling, immediately successive generation; the task of literary history is to reconsider and reclaim. In modernismo the roots of César Vallejo, Gabriela Mistral, Jorge Luis Borges, Octavio Paz, and Pablo Neruda are to be found, unmistakably; diachronic translation—translating with hindsight—makes these connections more visible, even inevitable. The sign of spiritual unrest, the nostalgia for harmony, the search for origins, and cultural and individual identity mark these spirits, who were a product of, and yet have transcended, their historical moment. Since too much perhaps has been made of modernismo's literary and cultural inheritance from Europe, the challenge before the reader is to see these works as transcultural products, and doubly so in English, or, in Manuel Gutiérrez Nájera's term, *intersecciones* ("intersections") (Scholz 136; Gutiérrez Nájera's term qtd. in Aparicio 34). The contemporaneity and originality of the modernistas are actually startling. For newcomers more familiar with the Anglo-American tradition, modernista poetry will prove full of inflections peculiar to the Romance languages: a self-conscious search in form and in language for transcendence; artifice without falsity (at least in its finest moments); and a range of identity concerns—the indigenous past, nationhood, the city, race, religion, aesthetics, exile, science—that shed light on, and complement, issues developing in other latitudes. We are heirs, we discover in modernista poetry, to the same disquiet inherent in modernity, to the same two poles between which modern poetry oscillates, poles that Paz called the magical and the revolutionary:

> The magical consists of a desire to return to nature by dissolving the self-consciousness that separates us from it, "to lose oneself forever in animal innocence, or liberate oneself from history." The revolutionary aspiration, on the other hand, demands a "conquest of the historical world and of nature." Both are ways of bridging the same gap and reconciling the "alienated consciousness" to the world outside.[1]

The approximate dates of Spanish American modernismo are from 1882, the appearance of José Martí's *Ismaelillo*, to 1916, the year of the death of the Nicaraguan poet and standard-bearer Rubén Darío, when the avant-garde movements—futurism, creationism, cubism, ultraism—were coming into vogue and reactions against modernismo were taking hold. Modernismo should not be confused with the Anglo-American movement modernism, begun in the 1910s, or with Brazilian modernismo, their avant-garde. Some critics date the inception of Spanish American modernismo strictly from Darío's *Azul* (1888; "Azure"). Modernismo was the first uniquely Spanish American literature, realizing the continent's desire both to join universal literature—aesthetic modernity—and to break colonial ties with the then-stagnant Spanish belles lettres.

Economic realities of the time unified the modernista writers. The rise of the bourgeoisie and the professionalization of the writer were key factors in the development of the modernista reaction. The mercantilist mentality inherited from positivism produced a backlash not only against realist and naturalist literature but also against the narrow utilitarian view of art's role in the societies preoccupied with the new accessibility of luxury goods—in other words, against the view of art as merely another commodity.

The artist was cut adrift. Where once poets were national spokespersons, heroes, lawgivers, and edifying voices behind nation building—as during Romanticism—now poets were disinherited, marginal figures, *poètes maudits* ("accursed poets") whose presence was unsettling to the bourgeois mind. Many modernistas wrote of jewels and Versaillesque palaces but actually led precarious economic lives, writing piecework for newspapers, holding government sinecures as functionaries or diplomats, or teaching (teaching was a low-paying job in Spanish America). In Darío's classic short story "El rey burgués" ("The Bourgeois King"), the poet is reduced in the end to turning the handle of a music box, is given one crust of bread per tune, and is paid *not* to recite; in short, the poet is silenced (and finally dies out in the cold).

Modernismo reclaimed the poetic vocation as a high calling in society, even as it fashioned utopian, nostalgic, or other contrarian visions that implicitly or explicitly rejected turn-of-the-century priorities. Meanwhile, with the artist's role in crisis, fin-de-siècle ailments of alienation—or "dis-association" in Saúl Yurkievich's term—were legion; the artist led, indeed, a double life of two irreconcilable forces (17), that of art from within and that of utility from without. As Julio Ramos describes at length in *Divergent Modernities*, the Spanish American writer at the time struggled against an uneven modernization, the crux of which was the problem of the autonomy of literary discourse—that is, the legitimacy and viability of the writing career. Seeming to tie this concept to Paz's two poles of modern poetry, Mike Gonzalez and David Treece note:

> The modernistas vacillated between Palladian visions of a world of culture outside time, in which the inequities of the actual world of Latin America were lost in the equality of artistic values, and a withdrawal into a despairing and enclosed self, which would ultimately be drained by its lack of renewal, its failure to draw any sustenance from the world of change. So this aristocracy of the spirit defined itself, in part, by its skeptical response to the optimistic historicism of the Positivists; for many different reasons they called into question the assumption that modernization and progress would be universally beneficial. (3; emphasis mine)

The artist's condition contrasted sharply with, and was possibly a consequence of, the aesthetic of robustness and health typical of progress-minded Victorian societies. In Europe and Latin America alike, the sick artist now was the model. Many artists embraced the very epithets that polite society hurled at them—for example, "decadence" became a way of sublimely distancing oneself from debased values; of creating artificial paradises in the senses (whether through art or drugs); hunting sensation; or celebrating perversity, irrationality, and the corrupted underside of civilization. The avatars of the disaffected artist were many: the dandy, the bohemian, the androgyne, the bon vivant, the neuropath, the neurasthenic, the splenetic, the café revolutionary, and the *rastaquoère* (the Spanish American expatriate in Europe, of uncertain means and status). The inner life (*reino interior* or "the kingdom within," as Darío called it) was valued; melancholy—an ambiguous and subtle state—was cultivated and indulged.

Consolation formerly found in consecrated thought systems was now available only in art, over which the priestly artist presided. Friedrich Nietzsche had provided the watchword: art is what justifies existence. Beauty was the new religion, and mystery recovered its ascendancy over dogmatic certainties. Old orthodoxies were retained, however, as repertoires of ideas from which the moderns could make syncretic new unions that were beautiful and strange: the secular and the religious, nostalgia and dread, East and West, the local and the cosmopolitan, the sensorial and the extrasensorial, the frivolous and the complicated, Whitmanian vitalism and morbid delectation.

At the same time—and here is one of the many contradictions that make modernismo still relevant and so susceptible to misunderstanding—the modernistas did not simply harmonize thoughts into pleasant reveries. The note of spiritual crisis, of dissonance, ran parallel and deep, particularly as modernismo entered the second decade of the twentieth century, a period of speed, war, and furious mechanization. This literary zeitgeist could produce wildly contrasting poetic discourses, like Darío's "A Roosevelt" ("To Roosevelt"), Leopoldo Lugones's "La blanca soledad" ("White Solitude"), and Gutiérrez Nájera's "To Be." Another paradox is that the modernistas' anguish often took the soberest of forms—chiseled rhymes and impeccable rhythms.

Ironic fracture—the ripples of blood in the noble swan's wake, in Delmira Agustini's memorable nocturne—would accompany modernismo to its end, and poetry was poised to shift from the imaginational toward the experiential, to turn "impure," as Neruda called his aesthetic goal; more elemental (poems about everyday things started appearing); and more transparently political, populist, and vernacular (with notable exceptions in the avant garde that were even more hermetic and dehumanized).

Coinage of the term *modernismo* is attributed to Darío (1888). Its aesthetics, politics, and legacy have been debated and studied now for over a century.[2] Modernismo was a nondogmatic current, as Orlando Gómez Gil indicates (405), acratic despite its aristocratic posturing, and not a movement or school as such but a moment or consciousness. Common denominators in any definition of modernismo are that it was a revolutionary spirit in Spanish America and later Spain; that it believed in the autonomy of art, the supremacy of beauty, and the cult of form. In rebelling against orthodoxies of all kinds, it liberated and renovated a dormant literature, making Spanish American belles lettres relevant internationally. The modernista sensibility can be said to include many of the following articles of faith:

> (a) a preoccupation with the marginalized status of the writer, and his or her fall from legislator to "non-producer"; at the same time, a recognition of the writer's interpretative role in the universe—the artist as shaman, magus, bard, artisan of the verbal object; (b) disdain for the acquisitiveness of the philistine classes and all that was admired by bourgeois values: the mass-marketed, accessible, emotionally dishonest, crass, commercial productions ruled by the judgments of the class Charles Baudelaire called the "mediocracy"; (c) art as a new source of faith; (d) language as incantatory, orphic, and the means to transgressing, transcending, and creating a "double" of the universe; (e) formal refinement and innovation; (f) an aspiration toward beauty, understood in a Platonic sense; (g) a cultivation of the vague and suggestive over the concrete, highlighting mystery, uncertainty, pessimism and ephemerality; (h) the awareness of Latin America as a presence emerging from exotic "Other" to exploited source of resources and victim of the foreign policies and cultural hegemony of colonial aggressors. (Washbourne 8–9)

Modernistas have long been accused of being apolitical or *torredemarfilista* ("ivory-tower-ist" or "elitist") or, to repeat a term that was the hobbyhorse of a certain kind of critic during much of the twentieth century, escapist, with all the cowardice the term implies. Modernista values, much to the contrary, countered the increasing threat of mercantalism and the secularization of modern life. Many writers of the day supported or promoted the material advancement of their countries but deplored the attendant materialism and problems of urbanization. An often overlooked dimension of modernista writing, ethics, reveals another key: the modernista extended the harmony of proportion to behavior. Aesthetics ruled ethics. An act was distasteful if it was discordant. A person's life, commensurately, was a person's own work of art.

In short, the modernistas were reacting against the loss of transcendence, of the sacred, of miraculousness in the world. Their intense inventiveness in form, imagery, allusiveness, and poetic personae may be seen as an attempt to restore wholeness, to create ideal worlds, alternative worlds.[3] Or, as Ivan Schulman suggests, the work of the modernista artist is as authentic and realistic as many of the imported forms of European realism, which failed to capture Spanish American realities and yet offered a—misleading—guise of truth (35). The modernistas' greatest nemesis was not reality but the prosaic, which their aesthetic ignored, scorned, or transmuted into beauty. Yet while modernista works apparently exercised exoticism for its own sake, close inspection often reveals that they historicized to a great extent. Note how Ricardo Jaimes Freyre's lyrical epics of Nordic myth are set against a backdrop of nascent Christianity ("Æternum vale"). Other works bore witness to the rise of North American militarism and expansionism (e.g., the Panama Canal and the Spanish-American War) or opposed the cult of United States cultural influence, *nordomanía* ("craze for the north"). Still others continued the Romantic tradition of the ode that constructs national identity. Darío's "Canto a la Argentina" ("Song to Argentina"), using an all-embracing utopian discourse, exalts the country's masses, the vibrancy of its immigration, its pampas, the promise of its future, and the creation of Continental and Anglo-Latin fellowship.

The notion that modernismo marked a retreat from the world arose in part from an error in criticism: an over-identification of certain works and writers with an apolitical agenda for all modernistas and an unquestioning reading of the voluptuous materiality of their images as a surrender to frivolity. Angel Rama describes in the chapter "The Polis Politicized" of his *The Lettered City* that though the writers concentrated as never before on their newly professionalized labor of writing,[4] most were committed to politics, wrote about it, and even participated in it, and the ancient belief that people of letters are best suited to govern held great sway in Latin American intellectual life at the time (77). Philosophical, ideological, and political leadership were avenues of social influence now at the forefront, and the modernistas' discourse even extended to a spiritual leadership role, that of secular "physicians of the spirit" who

> worked tenaciously to enhance the public dignity of intellectuals and even to cloak themselves in a sacred aura ("Towers of God! Poets!") as an antidote to the discordant materialism and spiritual bankruptcy of modern mass society. (78–79)

Darío in particular, from his earliest poems, explicitly set out to follow Victor Hugo's credo of poetic responsibility: a spiritual, political, and moral purposefulness (Jrade 85). For Martí, the whole liberational mission of the artist depended on redemption: "If spiritual freedom is not safeguarded, then literary originality has no place and political freedom does not long endure" (49). His writings and speeches combined "spiritualism, mystic nationalism, and compassion for the poor and abused" (González Echevarría xi). The modernista's political and spiritual impulses would find their most resounding expression in José Enrique Rodó's (1871–1917) polemic *Ariel* (1900) and his masterpiece, *Los motivos de Proteo* (1909; "The Motives of Proteus"), both works addressed to the youth of South America.

Self-conscious literariness and social commitment, then, proved not to be mutually exclusive for the modernista, even in the same writer's body of work, though the perception of "rubendarianismo"—an early misnomer for the modernista tradition—as apolitical persisted in the face of abundant evidence to the contrary. Examples abound: Manuel González Prada, whose extensive writings are now available in English, was a modernista and early anarchist and provides a clear example of engaged writing. José Santos Chocano was a revolutionary on a continental scale; he wrote blistering attacks from jail championing popular causes (though at times he would side with the structures of power, including dictatorships). As Paz notes, in the very name *modernismo* we see the writers' will to be contemporary and thus "to participate, intellectually, in the actions of history"—in other words, the desire to bring the local into the "universal present" of modernity, in Paz's phrase (*Siren* 23). A largely urban, transnational phenomenon, as Gerard Aching notes, modernismo grounded many of its discursive constructions in obvious class-related signifiers, but this practice was in fact strategic: to create a postcolonial cultural identity and express an experience of the modern by sifting, assimilating, and refashioning European cultural signs to forge an identity "from the periphery" (147–49). Significantly, then, a poem not overtly about politics may nonetheless be political. Paz rebukes critics who missed this point: "The charge of superficiality can be more justly leveled at those critics who could not read within the lightness and cosmopolitan spirit of the modernista poets the signs (the stigmata) of spiritual exile" (*Children* 59).

Modernismo appeared first in the northernmost regions of Spanish America, more or less simultaneously in Cuba, Mexico, and Colombia, and spread to virtually the entire Spanish-speaking world. It even influenced literature in Spain—for the first time in a significant way—and Spain's Generation of '98, a group of writers in existential and political crisis. Darío emerged early. The other major early figures are Martí, José Asunción Silva, Salvador Díaz Mirón, Julián del Casal, and Gutiérrez Nájera. Later appeared such writers as Julio Herrera y Reissig, Amado Nervo, Jaimes Freyre, Agustini, and Lugones. This second group became a vital link between modernista aesthetics and the avant-garde ruptures to come. The Peruvian Santos Chocano was important in the *mundonovista* ("new-world-ist") phase of modernismo, in which simplicity and the autochthonous prevailed over Europeanized, self-consciously artistic values. During this era, Darío's *Cantos de vida y esperanza* (1905; "Songs of Life and Hope") featured overtly political poems, especially dealing with North and South America, though Darío never abandoned his internationalist and universal scope or his belief in the redemptive power of art, as the title of his book implies.

A brief sketch of the women modernistas follows. Sylvia Molloy notes the difficulties for women writing at a time when the male gaze dismembered and objectified women in art (109), a gaze that ensures that "women cannot be, at the same time, inert textual objects and active authors" (qtd. in Escaja, "Invención" 141). Women, particularly in the early (pre-1900) phase of modernismo, were figured as muses, Ophelias, Salomés, Venuses, vampires, angels, mermaids, saints, Helens, hysterics, statues, witches, sirens, goddesses, Amazons, sphinxes, nymphs, corpses, courtesans, princesses, virgins, queens, harlots, geishas, cats, swans, and doves—rarely as flesh-and-blood women.[5]

Díaz Mirón's poem "Cleopatra" and José Juan Tablada's "Quinta Avenida" ("Fifth Avenue"), both included in this volume, provide case studies of this fetishizing impulse by which woman is always other. Or woman is reified: Gutiérrez Nájera's well-known "Para un menú" ("For a Menu") transforms woman into a "buffet" of intoxicating libations for an insatiable gourmand's table, while ex-lovers are "copas vacías" ("empty cups"). In Martí's "Amor de ciudad grande" ("Love in the City"), a woman becomes one more luxury possession, a bibelot. In Tablada's poem, women are pointedly mechanized, commercialized (the consumers and the consumed), their human sexuality placed in doubt (they are likened to bank safes all with the "idéntica combinación numérica" ["identical combination"]). The poem's narrator simultaneously exalts the unreachable, modern, independent woman, who has no use for the gazing flaneur, and demeans her, reading her indifference mockingly with the fantasy that her mode of reproduction is superhuman, exaggeratedly and inhumanly sexual. Mythologized woman is thus at once privileged and deprived. This tension of the age is captured in the poem's fifteen lines (the opening distich of which is deceptively romantic), while in the same stroke the impersonal modern city is implicated: capitalism as degradation. In Darío's poem "¡Carne, celeste carne de la mujer . . . !" ("Flesh, Heavenly Flesh of Woman . . . !"), the gender lines are even more clearly drawn: woman is mystery and muse, while man acts on her behalf and for her favor: "¡Toda lucha del hombre va a tu beso, / por ti se combate o se sueña!" ("All man's strife is bound for your kiss, / for you one fights and dreams!").

Charles Baudelaire's cruel judgment of women in "The Painter of Modern Life" (1863) represents a prevailing sentiment of the day: woman is

> that being as terrible and incommunicable as the Deity (with this difference, that the Infinite does not communicate because it would thereby blind and overwhelm the finite, whereas the creature of whom we are speaking is perhaps only incomprehensible because *it has nothing to communicate*). (30; emphasis mine)

Baudelaire illustrates the disassembling and artistic "manhandling" that artists perform on women: "[Woman] is not, I must admit, an animal whose component parts, correctly assembled, provide a perfect example of harmony" (30). In other words, the imperative of the artist—particularly in the decadent ethos—was to improve on nature; in this view, woman was something natural in need of organizing and heightening by means of cosmetics and art. It is no accident that since so many poems from the era cast women more as objets d'art than as subjects, women are usually silent. "Finding your voice" was no mere trope for the turn-of-the-century woman writer.

Work remains to be done on the exclusionary process of canon formation in modernismo, but it is clear that many women were not silent during the modernista era, despite their marginalization and misrepresentation; a few even wrote for literary journals or wrote entire books, sometimes under a pseudonym. Their reception at the time ranged from predictable, if sometimes subtle, condescension (Agustini was known as a child prodigy into adulthood) to outright hostility, since writing was not seen as a pursuit befitting a woman.

In the twenty-first century, we see that women's writing from this time often allows a dual reading, as both shared human experience and the expression of a specifically female consciousness. Agustini's "Lo inefable" ("The Ineffable"), for example, may be read beyond its topos of the angst of expression and extended to a gendered reading: a woman overcomes an imposed silence.[6] Today's readers should realize how subversive the inversion of the male gaze, a woman's expression of physical desire, was at the time, though many contemporary (male) critics deflected attention to other, more innocent aspects of women modernistas' work. Witness Borrero's "Apolo" ("Apollo"), in which the aesthetic object turns libidinous, or Vaz Ferreira's "Los desterrados" ("The Exiles"), in which the male body at work is seen erotically. The first-person voice in the second poem is that of a female wayfarer who is not the man's wife; thus the author was challenging the double standard of the day, which allowed the male libido to be expressed but not the female. Agustini liberates the mythologized woman in "El cisne" ("The Swan"), implicitly arguing that Leda is not a sexual victim. The silence of the poem's "I" is not passive; it "interrogates" and is "answered" with the swan lover's flesh.

Many modernistas, whether male or female, published few if any books in their lifetimes. Journals that published modernistas, however, were numerous and active. A few of the most important ones were, in Mexico, *Revista azul* (1894), edited by Gutiérrez Nájera; in Argentina, *Revista de América* (1894), edited by Darío and Jaimes Freyre, *Caras y caretas* (1898), a widely circulated magazine of both aesthetic and popular sensibility, and *El Mercurio de América* (1898); in Uruguay, *Revista nacional de literatura* (1895) and *La revista* (1899), edited by Herrera y Reissig; in Colombia, *Revista gris* (1892–96), edited by Max Grillo; and in Cuba, *La Habana elegante* (1883). Artist guilds such as Ateneo de Buenos Aires ("Buenos Aires Athenaeum") and, in Montevideo, Torre de los Panoramas ("Tower of Panoramas") and Consistorio del Gay Saber ("Town Hall of the Gay Science") were at the forefront of the new aesthetics.

Modernismo is known mostly for its poetry. Its prose has not yet received much attention, though it displayed many of the same traits and was vital to later developments in the genre (see A. González). Its lasting contributions include Martí's *Amistad funesta* (1885; "Ill-Fated Friendship"); Rodó's *Ariel*, which is a long moral reverie on spirit and matter and which contains one of the finest summations of modernista aesthetics, the parable of the "rey hospitalario" ("hospitable king"); some fine examples of the artist novel (Manuel Díaz Rodríguez's *Idolos rotos* [1901; "Broken Idols"] and Silva's *De sobremesa* [written in 1896 and published in 1925; *After-Dinner Conversation*]); *crónicas* ("chronicles," literally, but a hybrid genre[7] that was perhaps a prelude to Borges's curious *inquisiciones* or "inquisitions"); *transpositions d'art*, which translated one art form (e.g., painting) in terms of another (e.g., poetry); the short story, most notably by Darío and by Gutiérrez Nájera; and the children's tale (Martí's *La edad de oro* [1889; "The Golden Age"]).

Modernismo also created new genres based on the fine arts. In Julián del Casal's work, for example, we find *medallones* ("medallions"), *camafeos* ("cameos"), and *siluetas* ("silhouettes"). Elsewhere we find prose poems, a French innovation; vignettes; sketches; poems intended for *albums* (what in English were called scrap albums, memory books, or autograph albums, which were kept by educated young ladies in the nineteenth century, who embellished them with art, mementos, lithographs, or embroidery); poems composed on fans; and occasional poems to be read on the deaths of literary confreres or at *tertulias*—literary gatherings and recitals, a mainstay, then and now, of the Spanish American literary scene and vital to reputation making.

Metrically, the modernistas covered the gamut of possible forms, especially classical ones, or those imported from French models and reimagined. Alexandrines were common, as were hendecasyllables and even free verse. Experimentation was common with new strophic arrangements, rhythms, and line breaks (e.g., Silva's "Nocturno III" ["Nocturne III"], which the new aesthetes loved but was reviled by some traditionalists on its debut). This metric freedom took aim at the claustrophobic and academic aridity of earlier poetry, both from Spain and Latin America.

Two major foreign movements that left their mark on modernismo were symbolism and Parnassianism. Symbolism sought nuance, correspondences, and secret analogies as the highest goals of art. Highly spiritualized, it was an aesthetic that valued interiority and private vision. The post-Romantic phase of William Butler Yeats's poetry, for example, falls into this category, and the leaders of this current included Stephane Mallarmé and Paul Verlaine. Arthur Symons's landmark *The Symbolist Movement in Literature* (1899) details the poetics and international manifestations of the movement. Parnassianists, by contrast, sought to unite word and sound in a harmonious whole. Their influence on the modernistas is pronounced, especially in their cultivation of the sonnet form and their rejection of romantic effusiveness and sentimentality. They believed also in the concept of pure poetry, which aspired to create music with words stripped of all prosaism. Among the leaders of Parnassianism were Charles-Marie Leconte de Lisle and Théophile Gautier. Critics would seize on French forms and thematics to dismiss modernismo as a frenchified affectation, but in reality the Spanish Americans personalized and transformed these influences. From European Romanticism, modernismo inherited the issues of fragmentation, alienation, and the loss of premodern guarantees of knowledge (Jrade 3). The extent to which modernismo broke with Romanticism or furthered it, and in what ways, is still being debated.

Readers versed in the aestheticism of late-nineteenth-century England and the United States will find many points of comparison with modernismo. They will also find resonances of Edgar Allan Poe and Walt Whitman in these Spanish American texts, a presence that is well documented; although the presence of Whitman, at least, is a complicated matter of selective, belated, and distorted influence.[8] Modernism in the Anglo-American tradition, with which Ezra Pound and T. S. Eliot are strongly identified, emerged as modernismo was waning but shares its restless search for modernity, partly in things foreign. Both Pound and Tablada would discover Li Po, for example, and not coincidentally: Li Po's condensed image offered a counterpoint to the prolixity of modernista and Victorian styles, and both the Spanish American avant-gardes and the Anglo-American movements of imagism and vorticism embraced its possibilities.

The modernists in the United States drew differently from their poetic inheritance than did the modernistas:

> It was not until after 1914 that the generation of Pound, Eliot, Stevens, and Williams accomplished for the United States what the modernistas had accomplished for Spanish America. The U.S. modernists drew in large part on the same sources—French symbolist poetry—to effect their own break with their poetic past. In making this break, they made little use of their own poetic antecedents, Poe and Whitman. . . . (Chevigny and Laguardia 22)

Vallejo, Vicente Huidobro, and others in the avant-garde did not share the mostly conservative or reactionary politics of their Anglo-American contemporaries (Eliot and Pound in particular), but both currents embodied reactions against the realities of advanced capitalism, whether directly in the United States or indirectly in Spanish America (23).

In modernista aesthetics, poetry and the arts (music, painting, and sculpture) frequently appear as the subject. One manifestation is ekphrasis, the representation of the visual arts or art objects in poetry. Casal's sequence *Mi museo ideal* ("My Ideal Museum") re-creates works by the French painter Gustave Moreau, for example. Synesthesia, the blending of the senses, was believed to heighten the artistic effect (e.g., Darío's "Sinfonía en gris mayor" ["Symphony in Grey Major"]). We find poems that dramatize the role of the artist, some taking the form of counsel (Darío's "¡Torres de Dios!" ["Towers of God!"], González Martínez's "Busca en todas las cosas" ["Search Out in All Things"]) or placing the poet in the role of prophet, seer or inner visionary (Darío's "El reino interior" ["The Kingdom Within"]), or outcast (Eguren's "Peregrín cazador de figuras" ["Peregrine the Image Hunter"]). An ars poetica may declare the writer's conception of art (Silva's "Ars" ["Ars Poetica"], Martí's "Si ves un monte de espumas . . ." ["If you see a mountain of ocean spray . . ."] or "Contra el verso retórico" ["Against Rhetorical Poetry"], Darío's "Yo persigo una forma . . ." ["I Seek a Form . . ."]). Related themes are the crisis of expression (Agustini's "Lo inefable" ["The Ineffable"], Darío's "La página blanca" ["The Blank Page"]), the refined sensibility fleeing the commonness of the masses and their taste (Díaz Mirón's "Las orquídeas" ["Orchids"]), and the desire for transcendence in art and thought (Agustini's "Las alas" ["The Wings"]).

Modernista writing explores such subjects as beauty, eroticism, and desire, including the woman's point of view (Borrero's "Apolo" ["Apollo"], Agustini's "El intruso" ["The Intruder"]); sexual politics (Herrera y Reissig's "Decoración heráldica" ["Heraldic Decoration"], Vaz Ferreira's "Rendición" ["Surrender"]); nostalgia for the past (Silva's "Vejeces" ["Things Past"] and Eguren's "Marcha fúnebre de una Marionnette" ["Funeral March of a Marionette"], which revisits childhood fantasy); the city and the country (Martí's "Amor de ciudad grande" ["Love in the City"] and Casal's "En el campo" ["In the Country"]); death (Gutiérrez Nájera's "Para entonces" ["When

My Time Comes"], a poetic treatment of Walter Pater's mantra "to burn always with this hard, gemlike flame" [250], Lugones's "Historia de mi muerte" ["Story of My Death"], Silva's "Nocturno III" ["Nocturne III"], Jaimes Freyre's "Lo fugaz" ["Ephemera"], Nervo's "Al cruzar los caminos" ["At the Crossroads"], which adds the nuance of a death of individual consciousness); abnormal psychology (Gutiérrez Nájera's "Mis enlutadas" ["My Ladies in Mourning"], Silva's "El mal del siglo" ["*Mal du Siècle*"], Lugones's "A Histeria" ["To Hysteria"]); occultist doctrine (Darío's "En las constelaciones" ["In the Constellations"]); unrealities and other worlds (Jaimes Freyre's "Las voces tristes" ["The Doleful Cries"], Nervo's "Edelweiss," virtually all of Eguren's poetry); and finally historical and sociopolitical realities (the injustices recounted in Valencia's "Anarkos" ["Anarchos"], exile in Martí's "Dos patrias" ["Two Countries"], and the incarnation of a voice of South American nature and history in Santos Chocano's "Oda salvaje" ["Wild Ode"]).

The images and tropes one can expect to find in modernismo include religious icons placed in secular or syncretic, aestheticized contexts (temples, holy wafers, choirs, hymns); images from heraldry and nobility (viscounts, the fleur-de-lis); the swan, with its multiple possible readings as androgynous, ambiguous, pure, and aloof; the peacock; evocations of mental illness, derangement, and new modern ailments (neuralgia, nervous illness, neurosis); drugs (opium, hashish, laudanum); death (tombs, marble, shrouds); liminal worlds and objects (moonlit paths, wings, a city in midair, a nest of angels); primary colors (blue, white, black, red); nuanced colors and new adjectives for them (strawberry-and-cream, quicksilver, champagne); precious gems (diamond, pearl, amethyst); the vocabulary of interior decoration (silks, crystals, porcelain, crepe, fans, weaponry, all emphasizing lightness, beauty, or the archetypal, in opposition to the heaviness, ugliness, and reiterability of machines and the industrially produced); figures from fairy tales, legends, and lost worlds (goblets, fairies, princesses, horsemen, damsels, towers, lily pads); dreams, sleep, and the flight of the soul; music; flowers (lilies, roses); sensorial references, including smells (incense, perfumes) and tastes (kisses, wine, nectar); birds and insects, particularly where their names are rare and euphonic (*libélulas* ["dragonflies"], *bulbules* ["nightingales"]); nature, but highly stylized; and women, sometimes languid, often fatal, and always beautiful. Much of the imagery is derived from the stock of systems ancient (classical figures, mythology, alchemy, Rosicrucianism, paganism, orphism, hermeticism) and new (spiritism, modern science, theosophy). Finally, foreign words, archaisms, and recherché terms appear in abundance.

This volume contains the work of eighteen Spanish American modernista poets: seventy representative and pedagogically useful poems from that era. The collection emphasizes the poetry over the poets. The poets are presented in chronological order by birth year; each writer's poems are chronologically ordered by appearance in a published book or journal. The major writers, including those once considered precursors, are represented—Casal, Silva, Darío, Martí—but so too are writers lesser known or absent in English—Gutiérrez Nájera, Borrero, Jaimes Freyre, Santos Chocano, and Herrera y Reissig. The reader is invited to make an appraisal of the era that goes beyond the two or three figures who are usually considered at length, to the neglect of others. The criteria for our selection were the importance or relevance of a poem; the poem's potential effect in English (its translatability); its representativeness of a writer's oeuvre; thematic variety; poem length and form; the poem's relation to the canon or recent editions; and the poem's resonance with student readers of varying skill levels, tastes, and backgrounds in literature.

Older translations of modernismo—for example, Thomas Walsh's or Alice Stone Blackwell's in the 1920s, or G. Dundas Craig's in the 1930s—tended toward the ornamental, adding what in music are called appoggiaturas, grace notes that cut into the main notes' time without adding to the harmony or melody. The term is Italian for "leaning," an appropriate metaphor for what in translation is essentially a crutch: prettifying flourishes or trills, particularly those that serve rhyme above sense, a far easier goal than the reverse. Also, the ratio between concretion and abstraction in those older translations would be freely manipulated through padding to account for English's preference for specificity. These additions actually reduced a poem's dynamism by distorting and diluting emphasis, and the result was a digressionary version more than a translation. Another extreme approach—the plainspoken voice—would be equally dishonest in translating these poets. Instead, the goals in this volume are compression; rhythmic tension; and coherent, unencumbered lines—in short, poetry and not its paler incarnation, verse.

This project continues the critical challenge to the perception that modernismo was mere escapism or decorative art. The challenge draws attention not only to the reasons behind modernismo's aesthetics but also to its politically engaged writing and its spiritual-esoteric dimension. Also, three women writers are included here among their more canonically established male contemporaries. We encourage further research into the subject of women modernistas, so that more is brought to light about their role in the era's production. Most anthologies to date have depicted modernismo as an all-male club.

This anthology of modernismo, the first in bilingual format since the 1950s, is intended not as an exhaustive chronicle of the era but as a usable, level-appropriate introduction for upper-division undergraduate literature students or graduate students in fields such as Spanish and comparative literature. This book was designed with the student in mind, to be used to best advantage in classroom readings and discussion.

For reasons of space, we could not include certain poets and poems: for example, work by Manuel González Prada (1848–1918); the early work of Luis Llorens Torres (1876–1944); Santos Chocano's indigenist "¡Quién sabe!" ("Who Knows?"), part of a trilogy that shows sympathy for the plight of Amerindians under colonial exploitation; long poems by Darío, such as "Canción de otoño en primavera" ("Song of Autumn in Spring"); more major poems by Gutiérrez Nájera, such as "Non Omnis Moriar" ("I Shall Not Die Altogether") and "La Duquesa Job" ("Duchess Job"); more women writers; perhaps a whole selection of important programmatic prologues by modernistas, including Lugones, Martí, and Darío; and more offerings by Martí, particularly his major poems still awaiting English translation as of this writing, such as "Homagno" ("The Great Man") and "Hierro" ("Steel").

In the translations in this volume, punctuation, spelling, and formatting of source texts are followed strictly, even when idiosyncratic, except for two modernizations: accents (e.g., *fue* for *fué*) and the noncapitalization of initial words of a verse. Spelling variations to maintain meter (e.g., "älas" for "alas" in Silva's "Nocturno III") are the authors'.

We wish to thank the editorial staff and consultant readers at MLA for this opportunity and for their valued suggestions and corrections.

Notes

[1]Qtd. in Hamburger 40. Paz concludes that the end of alienation would mean the end of language.

[2]One of the earliest and most important interpreters of modernismo was Pedro Henríquez Ureña, who delivered a series of lectures on it at Harvard in the early 1940s. See his *Corrientes literarias* and *Ensayos*. See also Max Henríquez Ureña. For a classic text from the second half of the twentieth century, see Jiménez.

[3]See Jrade in particular for more on the idea of the fragmented self and lost wholeness.

[4]Rama studied the economics of the modernistas in the marketplace in *Los poetas modernistas en el mercado económico* (1967). He described the writers' passage from the patronage system to their insertion into the market economy, where artistic production was not accorded an exchange value, few publishers were publishing, and no unions or other protections for the writers yet existed.

[5]A Jungian approach would make a revealing study of the depictions of women by male modernistas. Carl Jung saw anima figures as projections of the male's unrealized unconscious feminine aspects.

[6]Molloy posits the poem's central image of the head of God as one of childbirth and "wonderment at the birthing of the near monstrous," hence the overlapping semantic fields of pain, womanhood, silence, and communication, a highly productive reading (116–18). Escaja has seen in it the integration of the myth of Ophelia with the myth of Orpheus's dismemberment, forging the metaphor of sexual and linguistic wholeness ("[Auto] Creación"; qtd. in Cáceres 17). Varas reads the poem partly in Freudian terms: the creative act is a transgressive act of violence and perceived as immodestly ambitious for a woman writer (167).

[7]Martin defines the chronicle as "word poem, art reportage, interview converted into narrative, imaginative or literary essay, life of a writer, review of a book . . . , disguised brief narrative or travel tale," among other subgenres, perhaps including political editorial as well (69). For more on the emergence of the modernista chronicle, see Rotker, ch. 3.

[8]For more on the connection with Whitman, see Santí; Alegría.

Works Cited

Aching, Gerard. *The Politics of Spanish American Modernismo: By Exquisite Design*. New York: Cambridge UP, 1997.

Alegría, Fernando. "Whitman in Spain and Latin America." *Walt Whitman and the World*. Ed. Gay Wilson Allen and Ed Folsom. Iowa City: U of Iowa P, 1995. 71–127.

Allen, Esther, trans. and ed. *José Martí: Selected Writings*. New York: Penguin, 2002.

Aparicio, Frances R. *Versiones, interpretaciones, creaciones: Instancias de la traducción literaria en Hispanoamérica en el siglo veinte*. Gaithersburg: Hispamérica, 1991.

Baudelaire, Charles. *"The Painter of Modern Life" and Other Essays*. Trans. Jonathan Mayne. London: Phaidon, 1964.

Blackwell, Alice Stone, trans. *Some Spanish-American Poets*. Philadelphia: U of Pennsylvania P, 1929.

Cáceres, Antonio. *The Selected Poetry of Delmira Agustini: Poetics of Eros*. Ed. and trans. Alejandro Cáceres. Carbondale: Southern Illinois UP, 2003.

Chevigny, Bell Gale, and Gari Laguardia, eds. *Reinventing the Americas: Comparative Studies of Literature of the United States and Spanish America*. Cambridge: Cambridge UP, 1986.

Craig, G. Dundas, ed. and trans. *The Modernist Trend in Spanish-American Poetry*. Berkeley: U of California P, 1934.

Darío, Rubén. "El rey burgués." *Antología crítica de la prosa modernista hispanoamericana*. Ed. José Olivio Jiménez and A. de la Campa. New York: Torres, 1976. 90–95.

Escaja, Tina. "(Auto) Creación y revisionismo en *Los cálices vacíos* de Delmira Agustini." *Bulletin of Hispanic Studies* 75 (1998): 213–28.

———. "Invención de una periferia: Poetas hispanoamericanas de la modernidad." *Actas del XXX Congreso del Instituto Internacional de Literatura Iberoamericana*. Pittsburgh: Instituto Internacional de Literatura Iberoamericana, 1995. 137–42.

Gómez Gil, Orlando. *Historia de la literatura hispanoamericana*. New York: Holt, Rinehart, 1968.

González, Aníbal. *La novela modernista hispanoamericana*. Madrid: Gredos, 1987.

Gonzalez, Mike, and David Treece. *The Gathering of Voices: Twentieth-Century Poetry of Latin America*. London: Verso, 1992.

González Echevarría, Roberto. "José Martí: An Introduction." Allen ix–xxvi.

Hamburger, Michael. *The Truth of Poetry: Tensions in Modern Poetry from Baudelaire to the 1960s*. Rev. ed. Manchester, Eng.: Carcanet, 1983.

Henríquez Ureña, Max. *Breve historia del modernismo*. México: Fondo de Cultura Económica, 1954.

Henríquez Ureña, Pedro. *Las corrientes literarias en la América hispánica*. México: Fondo de Cultura Económica, 1949. Trans. of *Literary Currents in Hispanic America*.

———. *Ensayos en busca de nuestra expresión*. Buenos Aires: Raigal, 1952.

Jiménez, José Olivio, ed. *Antología crítica del modernismo*. Madrid: Hiperión, 1994.

Jrade, Cathy Login. Modernismo, *Modernity, and the Development of Spanish American Literature*. Austin: U of Texas P, 1998.

Martí, José. "Prologue to Juan Antonio Pérez Bonalde's *Poem of Niagara*." Allen 43–51.

Martin, Gerald. "Literature, Music, and the Visual Arts, 1870–1930." *A Cultural History of Latin America: Literature, Music, and the Visual Arts in the Nineteenth and Twentieth Centuries*. Ed. Leslie Bethell. New York: Cambridge UP, 1998. 47–130.

Molloy, Sylvia, ed. *Women's Writing in Latin America: An Anthology*. Boulder: Westview, 1991.

Neruda, Pablo. "Toward an Impure Poetry." *Selected Poems of Pablo Neruda*. Ed. and trans. Ben Belitt. New York: Grove, 1961. 39–40.

Pater, Walter Horatio. Conclusion. *The Renaissance*. London: Macmillan, 1888. 246–52.

Paz, Octavio. *Children of the Mire: Modern Poetry from Romanticism to the Avant-Garde*. Trans. Rachel Phillips. Cambridge: Harvard UP, 1974.

———. *"The Siren and the Seashell" and Other Essays on Poets and Poetry*. Trans. Lysander Kemp and Margaret Sayers Peden. Austin: U of Texas P, 1976.

Rama, Angel. *The Lettered City*. Ed. and trans. John Charles Chasteen. Durham: Duke UP, 1996.

———. *Los poetas modernistas en el mercado económico*. Montevideo: U de la República, 1967.

Ramos, Julio. *Divergent Modernities: Culture and Politics in Nineteenth-Century Latin America*. Trans. John D. Blanco. Durham: Duke UP, 2001.

Rotker, Susana. *The American Chronicles of José Martí: Journalism and Modernity in Spanish America.* Trans. Jennifer French and Katherine Semler. Hanover: UP of New England, 2000.

Santí, Enrique Mario. "The Accidental Tourist: Walt Whitman in Latin America." *Do the Americas Have a Common Literature?* Ed. Gustavo Pérez Firmat. Durham: Duke UP, 1990. 156–76.

Scholz, László. "Translation as a Literary Institution." Trans. Colman Hogan. Valdés and Kadir 2: 129–38.

Schulman, Ivan A. "Modernismo / modernidad: Metamórfosis de un concepto." *Nuevos asedios al modernismo.* Madrid: Taurus, 1987. 11–38.

Symons, Arthur. *The Symbolist Movement in Literature.* London: Heinemann, 1899.

Valdés, Mario J., and Djelal Kadir, eds. *Literary Cultures of Latin America: A Comparative History.* 3 vols. New York: Oxford UP, 2004.

Varas, Patricia. *Las máscaras de Delmira Agustini.* Montevideo: Vintén, 2002.

Walsh, Thomas, ed. *Hispanic Anthology: Poems Translated from the Spanish by English and North American Poets.* New York: Putnam, 1920.

Washbourne, Kelly. "Translator's Introduction: 'An Art Both Nervous and New.'" *After-Dinner Conversation.* By José Asunción Silva. Trans. Washbourne. Austin: U of Texas P, 2005. 1–48.

Yurkievich, Saúl. *La movediza modernidad.* Madrid: Taurus, 1996.

SUGGESTIONS FOR FURTHER READING

Agustini, Delmira. *Selected Poetry of Delmira Agustini: Poetics of Eros.* Ed. and trans. Alejandro Cáceres. Carbondale: Southern Illinois UP, 2003.

Bell-Villada, Gene. *Art for Art's Sake and Literary Life: How Politics and Markets Helped Shape the Ideology and Culture of Aestheticism, 1790–1990.* Lincoln: U of Nebraska P, 1996.

Benjamin, Walter. *Charles Baudelaire: A Lyric Poet in the Era of High Capitalism.* Trans. Harry Zohn. Ed. Hannah Arendt. New York: Schocken, 1969.

Bethell, Leslie, ed. *A Cultural History of Latin America.* New York: Cambridge UP, 1998.

Brotherston, Gordon, ed. *Spanish American Modernista Poets: A Critical Anthology.* 2nd ed. London: Bristol Classical; Newburyport: Focus Information Group, 1995.

Franco, Jean. *The Modern Culture of Latin America: Society and the Artist.* London: Pall Mall, 1967.

Jrade, Cathy Login. "Modernist Poetry." *Cambridge History of Latin American Literature.* Ed. Roberto González Echevarría and Enrique Pupo-Walker. Vol. 2. Cambridge: Cambridge UP, 1996. 7–68.

———. *Rubén Darío and the Romantic Search for Unity: The Modernist Recourse to Esoteric Tradition.* Austin: U of Texas P, 1983.

Kirkpatrick, Gwen. *The Dissonant Legacy of Modernismo: Lugones, Herrera y Reissig, and the Voices of Modern Spanish American Poetry.* Berkeley: U of California P, 1989.

———. Introduction. *Selected Writings.* By Leopoldo Lugones. Trans. Sergio Waisman. Lib. of Latin Amer. New York: Oxford UP, forthcoming.

Lugones, Leopoldo. *Strange Forces: The Fantastic Tales of Leopoldo Lugones.* Trans. Gilbert Alter-Gilbert. Pittsburgh: Latin Amer. Literary Rev., 2001.

Martí, José. *Selected Writings.* Trans. and ed. Esther Allen. New York: Penguin, 2002.

Molloy, Sylvia. "Introduction: Female Textual Identities: The Strategies of Self-Figuration." *Women's Writing in Latin America: An Anthology.* Ed. Molloy. Boulder: Westview, 1991. 105–24.

Paz, Octavio. *Children of the Mire: Modern Poetry from Romanticism to the Avant-Garde.* Trans. Rachel Phillips. Cambridge: Harvard UP, 1974.

———. *"The Siren and the Seashell" and Other Essays on Poets and Poetry.* Trans. Lysander Kemp and Margaret Sayers Peden. Austin: U of Texas P, 1976.

Rodo, José Enrique. *The Motives of Proteus.* Trans. Angel Flores. New York: Brentano's, 1928.

Varas, Patricia. "Pre-Raphaelite Female Imagery in Spanish American Poetry." *Victorian Review* 30.1. (2004): 72–91.

Wilson, Edmund. *Axel's Castle: A Study of the Imaginative Literature of 1870–1930.* New York: Scribner's, 1931.

PRIMARY TEXTS

Agustini, Delmira. *Poesías completas.* Ed. Alejandro Cáceres. Montevideo: Plaza, 1999.

Borrero, Juana. *Poesías y cartas.* Havana: Arte y Literatura, 1978.

Casal, Julián del. *Poesías completas y pequeños poemas en prosa en orden cronológico.* Ed. Esperanza Figueroa. Miami: Universal, 1993.

Darío, Rubén. *Obras completas.* Ed. V. M. Sanmiguel Raimúndez. Madrid: Afrodisio Aguado, 1950.

Díaz Mirón, Salvador. *Poesía completa.* Ed. Manuel Sol. Mexico City: Fondo de Cultura Económica, 1997.

Eguren, José María. *Obras completas.* Ed. Ricardo Silva-Santisteban. Peru: Centenario; Banco de Crédito del Perú, 1997.

González Martínez, Enrique. *Obras completas.* Ed. Antonio Castro Leal. Mexico City: Colegio Nacional, 1971.

Gutiérrez Nájera, Manuel. *Poesía.* Ed. Angel Muñoz Fernández. Mexico City: Factoria, 2000.

Herrera y Reissig, Julio. *Poesía completa y prosas.* Ed. Angeles Estévez. Madrid: Galaxia Gutenberg; Círculo de Lectores, 1999.

Jaimes Freyre, Ricardo. *Poesías completas.* La Paz: Ministerio de Educación y Bellas Artes, 1957.

Lugones, Leopoldo. *Obras completas.* Ed. Pedro Luis Barcia. Buenos Aires: Pasco, 1999.

Martí, José. *Poesía completa.* Ed. Carlos Javier Morales. Madrid: Alianza, 1995.

Nervo, Amado. *Poesías completas.* Barcelona: Teorema, 1982.

Santos Chocano, José. *Obras completas.* Ed. Luis Alberto Sánchez. Mexico City: Aguilar, 1954.

Silva, José Asunción. *Obra completa.* Ed. Héctor H. Orjuela. Madrid: CEP de la Biblioteca Nacional, 1990.

Tablada, José Juan. *Obras.* Ed. Héctor Valdés. Mexico City: UNAM, 1971–81.

Valencia, Guillermo. *Obra poética.* Ed. Pedro Gómez Valderrama. Bogotá: Círculo de Lectores, 1984.

Vaz Ferreira, María Eugenia. *Poesías completas.* Ed. Hugo Verani. Montevideo: Plaza, 1986.

NOTE ON THE TRANSLATIONS

The only true motive for putting poetry into a fresh language must be to endow a fresh nation, as far as possible, with one more possession of beauty.

—*Dante Gabriel Rossetti, preface to* The Early Italian Poets

[T]he poem dies when it has no place to go.

—*Eliot Weinberger,* Nineteen Ways of Looking at Wang Wei

Aims of Translation

A translation promises not a destination or a view but a vehicle.

Each metaphor for translation tells part of the story. A favorite metaphor is the translator as actor. Translators themselves too often turn this trope into the trope of the poor player: the translator, in the introduction, has long assumed the role of the understudy taking the stage to apologize to a crowd for the absence of the name actor. But translation as interpretation, as performance, even as celebration (whether reverent or carnivalesque) need make no apologies for what it does not pretend to be or do. Any text, even a deficient one—sometimes *because* it is deficient—may be a pre-text for some future text, and this is the way literature is transmitted, adapted, revitalized. Translation creates readers as it creates new texts. To use an organic metaphor, it is part of the cross-pollinization of culture. The translator as apologist incorrectly assumes that the translation cannot serve some useful end, offer some stimulus, provide some access. We gain from interpretations—musical, artistic, academic—as much as from our experience with the original source. And some arts need interpretation. Where does Mozart reside, except in interpretations? Who are authors, if readers, anthologists, editors, critics, and translators are not making and remaking them? Literature must have interpretation to remain vital. A translation of a poem must interpret, and it should yield a new poem; beyond these two basic truths, schools and schisms form. Kenneth Rexroth articulates, almost in passing, what could serve as a guiding precept for poetry translators: "I have never tried to explain away the poem, to translate the elusive into the obvious" (xxi).[1] Indeed, it is a lifelong pursuit to learn to let an object of one's craft take shape under one's hands without bending it to one's will.

Readers of this volume in the MLA series Texts and Translations may be inspired, as they confront otherness, to learn more Spanish, to compare the products of other national literatures, to write modernista-influenced poems to find their voice as creative writers, to seek out and study the precursors of these works, and even to attempt translations of their own—all welcome developments, to be sure. Occasionally, a translation may foreground some feature that even the specialist has not seen or heard. Reading translations as translations can provide a critical tool for close reading, opening up ways into how a poem means. Thankfully, renderings will be found here that challenge cherished interpretations. And so the ongoing dialogue with the works is unbroken.

A translator should be humble, true, but a translator's humility should not be proved in apologies.

Considerations of Context in Translating Modernismo in the Twenty-First Century

Ours is an age that rejects origins and originality, and yet there is an intolerance of copying the past. André Malraux has pointed out, "We do not mind a Rembrandt looking modern, but resent a modern picture looking like a Rembrandt." He reasons that the artist who reproduces is painting an "outer landscape" and that such a work follows not from the inner realm but from the scientist's method for apprehending perceptual reality. As he concludes, "The method of art is to change our inner experience so that we then perceive the perceptual world (and our inner experience) differently" (qtd. in LeShan 185). The faulty assumption behind this formulation is that a text from the past is a fixed, discrete entity. In fact, we are apt to see it now as a moving target, interpretable in countless, sometimes mutually exclusive, ways. Think of Don Quixote: to the Romantics, he was a Romantic; to the existentialists, an existentialist; to the revolutionaries, a revolutionary. Malraux's statement reveals another misapprehension: that art is simply an unmediated picture of some private, inner realm, a magic lantern show of the creator's thoughts.

The modernistas exist in a realm we might call the always already translated. Octavio Paz says, "Between the language of the universe and the universe of language, there is a bridge, a link: poetry. The poet, says Baudelaire, is the translator. The universal translator and the translator of the universe" (Honig 157). That is, if nature is already writing, all human writing is rewriting. Modernistas, apart from assuming this role as decipherers, inhabit a translational world of deeply inscribed international models, at a time that the concepts of author and authorship were becoming more liberally defined.[2] The modernista idea of translation included versions, re-creations, the inclusion of anglicisms, barbarisms, foreign forms, and in general an internationally centripetal energy. Even the many modernista *transpositions d'art*—which are intersemiotic translations—attest to this impetus to absorb, recast, and interpret. And of course, many of these writers were translators themselves. A very partial list of modernista translators and their translated authors follows:

Darío: Hugo, Lautréamont
Valencia: Keats, Mallarmé, Flaubert, D'Annunzio, Baudelaire
González Martínez: Heredia, Verlaine, Samain
Martí: Hugo
Lugones: Homer (*Iliad*)
Herrera y Reissig: Samain, Baudelaire
Casal: Gautier
Silva: Hugo, Beranger
Gutiérrez Nájera: Coppée, Hugo, Musset
Tablada: Li Po, Moréas, Heredia, Baudelaire
[Leopoldo] Diaz: Zola, Leconte de Lisle, D'Annunzio, Poe

In turn many of the modernistas were avid consumers of translations, including of Poe, which they read in Baudelaire's French, and of Whitman in Spanish.

Procedures and Strategies

Here are some lines by José María Eguren in my English translation (from "Peregrine the Image Hunter"):

> In imagination's lookout
> in the twinkling of perfume
> quivering harmonic;
> in the flame-devoured night,
> when the unfledged duck is sleeping,
> the Orphic insects throng,
> and the fireflies flare and dim; . . .

I often pare down adverbs into adjectives ("quivering harmonically" becomes "quivering harmonic") to demechanize the comfortable relation between a verb and its modifier and to avoid rhythmic infelicities—adverbs, like adjectives, can sap the life from a poem. The last line of the Spanish in this sample is "y luciérnagas fuman," which gives the image of insects smoking (inferentially, tobacco). Or the image of a firefly's intermittent light, like the tip of a lit cigarette in the dark that intensifies when the cigarette is inhaled. The smoking part of the analogy is not operative, only the cigarette's glowing tip. Ergo: "the fireflies flare and dim" (resolved in part by a technique known as compensation by splitting, which in this case creates two verbs in temporal succession).

In this collection I have used some mildly archaizing techniques in the interest of creating mood (tone) and of laying bare certain modernista devices: postpositing adjectives; hyperbaton and anastrophe; frequent compound adjectives (more common to the eighteenth century); and, in diction, the use of a considered balance of Romance and Anglo-Saxon words. I have often turned Spanish hendecasyllables into limping iambic lines, using a "ghost of a metre" in T. S. Eliot's phrase (36). "Christian" forms (∪/∪/) frequently substitute for the "pagan" forms that use a resolute first syllable, in Robert Bly's terminology. Bear in mind that English metrics are measured in feet, while Spanish poetry measures syllables. Bly's prescription for creating accessibility through vernacular translation would be misguided for rendering these eighteen writerly poets. Archaizing should be seen as a range, a kind of in-betweenness, hybrid, or compromise, given that United States English tends to resist the outright solemn, heroic, or high-flown registers. Translation theory is full of words that suggest this negotiability: *compensation*, for example, implies a repayment. Instead of speaking of what is lost in translation, we might consider losses temporary debts to be repaid elsewhere—and not necessarily in kind—in the same work or, more abstractly, in the sum of translations of that work. The foreignizing impulse—making strange or not familiarizing the strange—in translating modernismo can create an idiom contemporary with no one ideal reader, since preserving both contemporaneities (source and target) is impossible or undesirable. In *After Babel*, George Steiner calls for translation to "retain a *vital strangeness* and 'otherness' " (67; emphasis mine).

Translations of modernismo are akin to grafts: living tissues from different plants, united. This approach presupposes that the translator keeps an eye to what is living in the source text (the "vital" in Steiner's "vital strangeness"). In practice, the same dynamics applies as for lexical borrowing. Compare John Dryden's line: "I trade both with the living and the dead, for the enrichment of our native Language" (lxiv). The translator's reconstructive art reveals literature to be a product of effects, artifice, rhetorical strategies used to heighten and organize perceptual reality. Poe in "Philosophy of Composition" (1846) desacralizes the aura of the original by showing literary creation to be not inspiration but artifice, procedure, not "fine frenzy" but vacillation, trial and error, deliberateness. In his portrait of a demythified author we see the outlines of the demythified translator.

Even in the poem "El reino interior" ("The Kingdom Within"), Rubén Darío, while vaunting the inner life, relies on a whole processional of literary traditions: the *selva sagrada* ("sacred wood") where real and ideal coexist, the mystical number 7, the conceit of the artist as a captive in an enchanted space, the allegory of virtue and vice (complete with Verlainean Satans and Boticellean snowy virgins), and the topos of the aesthetic allure of sin. Thus, even inner experience appears (inter)textually—that is, wrought of a social vocabulary of conceits and devices. The translator's aim, like the author's, is to create "rosas artificiales que huelen a primavera" ("artificial roses that smell of spring"), in Darío's phrase ("De Catulle Mendés" 31).

Rhyme has not been preserved in these translations, on the grounds that the semiotics of rhyme has changed. Once rhyme was didactic, comforting, and analogical, but today, except in very skilled hands (Richard Wilbur comes to mind), it can too easily sound mechanical, infantile, or forced. I wrote the first draft of Casal's "Flowers of Ether" in pentameter; the effect was starchy. Invariably I turned to unmeasured rhythm. Rhythm may offer a translation of rhyme, in that they are analogues of each other, prelinguistic sound patterns with internal correspondences. Darío expressed the thought that poetry's music is often in the idea ("La música es sólo de la idea, muchas veces") and that each verse has a verbal harmony and a conceptual melody (*Páginas* 59).

Translated texts themselves may be kinds of harmony to the source texts' original, and even inharmonic translations may have their place. Whatever the strategy used, a danger always lies in assuming there is a ready-made poetic idiom. The uniqueness of a writer's voice is elusive and demands that preconceptions be set aside. As Martí writes, "Victor Hugo no escribe en francés . . . Víctor Hugo escribe en Víctor Hugo" (20; "Victor Hugo does not write in French . . . Victor Hugo writes in Victor Hugo"). The theorist André Lefevere believed that translation must go beyond analogy, where it starts, to see the source text clearly. He writes, "When we no longer translate Chinese T'ang poetry 'as if' it were Imagist blank verse, which it manifestly is not, we shall be able to begin to understand T'ang poetry on its own terms" (78). Translation must negotiate two worldviews and the passage of the work into a new ethos, grammar, and literary history. Any great work will violate norms and embody particularities that curmudgeons have taken to calling untranslatable. The doctrine of untranslatability often depends on fallacious premises—a too-narrow definition of translation or the nationalistic pride that denies the affiliation of any text outside its author's source language.

Lexically, a few specific examples may be offered to show how a translation can use contemporary intertexts and parallel texts that activate resonances available in the reader's experience. In Silva's "Nocturne III," the locution "every fiber of your frame" is an echo of Poe's "every fibre of my frame," from his short story "The Black Cat." For "*amarguras infinitas*" I found a certain affinity in

Samuel Taylor Coleridge's oneiric "Kubla Khan": bitternesses "measureless [to man]." "Measureless" somewhat personalizes the horror of the feeling: "infinite" is more conceptual than visceral and would frustrate the rhythmic scheme in English. I rendered Silva's nocturne using internal, assonant rhymes that accented long *o*, *a*, and *u* sounds to evoke mourning, and its famous form was transferred, its metrics measured strictly in multiples of four, as in Silva's original. I followed a tetrameter with an occasional trochee (stressed initial syllable in a foot). Coleridge, incidentally, used the tetrameter, as did Emerson in "Brahma": "They reckon ill who leave me out; / When me they fly, I am the wings; / I am the doubter and the doubt, / and I the hymn the Brahmin sings." Critics have noted the affinity of "Nocturno III" with Poe's "The Bells" (1849), whose syncopations prefigure Silva's: "They are neither man nor woman— / They are neither brute nor human— / They are Ghouls: / And their king is it who tolls."

Two bedeviling lines in this book came in Gutiérrez Nájera's "Para entonces" ("When My Time Comes"): "cuando la vida dice aún: soy tuya, / aunque sepamos bien que nos traiciona!" The implication of an unfaithful woman lies in the feminine adjective *tuya*; in the English I made her explicit so as not to lose the male narrator's bitter connection between life and women: "When life like a woman still says: I'm yours, / though well we know she'll be untrue." "Untrue" happily gained the two meanings of duplicitous and false, but the unambiguous introduction of the simile explained too much. In revision the lines were amended and shifted to the passive voice for the sake of rhythm: "when life still says: I'm yours, / though well we know we'll be betrayed!"

The overwhelming tendency toward domestication in United States translation publishing practices demonstrably affects the translator. The pattern of ready consumability or digestability of foreign texts makes any strange text have to fight for legitimacy. And we must factor in an incongruity: a cultural chasm yawns between the Anglo-American tradition, which favors "natural language," and in which word use is economical, transparent, and functional, and the Spanish American, where the traditions of the baroque and neobaroque have forged in language a virtuoso tool of lush proliferation and lyrical art.

Modernistas will go beyond their countries' borders as never before; modernismo's afterlife grows ever longer, wider, and more unpredictable as readers, critics, and translators read and reread, putting poetry in new forms and to new purposes. Modernismo lies worlds apart from us. Its translation is an *invitation au voyage*. The ready passenger will not mistake the vehicle for the view.

Sergio Waisman is the translator of the following poems: by Leopoldo Lugones, "To Hysteria," "Sullen Delights," "Lunar Digressions"; by Julio Herrera y Reissig, "Return from the Fields," "Neurasthenia"; by Delmira Agustini, "The Intruder," "The Wings," "Nocturnal," "The Swan." All the other poems in the volume were translated by Kelly Washbourne.

Notes

[1]It is this philosophy and not Rexroth's actual translation practices that I am holding up for emulation—I am aware of his incursions into the gray area of pseudotranslation (e.g., see Apter).

[2]See Aparicio, ch. 2, esp. 66. Aparicio provides much of the following list of modernistas and their translated authors.

Works Cited

Aparicio, Frances R. *Versiones, interpretaciones, creaciones: Instancias de la traducción literaria en Hispanoamérica en el siglo veinte.* Gaithersburg: Hispamérica, 1991.

Apter, Emily. "Translation with No Original: Scandals of Textual Reproduction." *Nation, Language, and the Ethics of Translation.* Ed. Sandra Bermann and Michael Wood. Princeton: Princeton UP, 2005. 159–74.

Bly, Robert. *The Eight Stages of Translation.* Boston: Rowan Tree, 1983.

Darío, Rubén. "De Catulle Mendès: Parnasianos y decadentes." 1888. *El modernismo y otros ensayos.* Ed. Iris M. Zavala. Madrid: Alianza, 1989. 31–33.

———. *Páginas escogidas.* Madrid: Cátedra, 1991.

Dryden, John. "The Translator's Introduction." *Virgil: The Aeneid.* New York: Heritage, 1944. i–lxviii.

Eliot, T. S. "Reflections on 'Vers Libre.'" *Selected Prose of T. S. Eliot.* Ed. Frank Kermode. New York: Harcourt, 1975. 32–38.

Honig, Edwin. "Octavio Paz: Interview." *The Poet's Other Voice: Conversations on Literary Translation.* Amherst: U of Massachusetts P, 1985. 153–63.

Lefevre, André. "Composing the Other." *Post-colonial Translation.* Ed. Susan Bassnett and Harish Trivedi. London: Routledge, 1999. 75–94.

LeShan, Lawrence. *Einstein's Space and Van Gogh's Sky: Physical Reality and Beyond.* New York: Macmillan, 1982.

Martí, José. "Traducir *Mes fils.*" *Martí traductor de Victor Hugo.* Ed. Camilo Carrancá y Trujillo. Mexico City: Talleres gráficos de la nación, 1933. 17–26.

Poe, Edgar Allan. "Philosophy of Composition." *Graham's Magazine* Apr. 1846: 163–67. Rpt. in *Poe's Essays, Sketches, and Lectures.* Edgar Allan Poe Soc. of Baltimore. 15 Jan 2006. 27 Sept. 2006 <http://www.eapoe.org/works/essays/philcomp.htm>.

Rexroth, Kenneth. *One Hundred Poems from the Japanese.* New York: New Directions, 1984.

Steiner, George. *After Babel: Aspects of Language.* Oxford: Oxford UP, 1998.

An Anthology of Spanish American Modernismo

José Martí

Revolutionary patriot, essayist, orator, and poet, José Martí (1853–95), the apostle of Cuban independence, is today a hero to exiles from the island nation and Communist adherents alike. Martí was the embodiment of the soldier-poet, devoted to both action and contemplation. Natural but no mere nature poet, he was heavily influenced by Krausism, which held that nature has a moral force and that humanity is in consonance with the universe. The Cuban especially espoused the Rousseauian belief in human perfectibility. As he would write in the first canto of *Versos sencillos* ("Simple Verses"): "Todo es hermoso y constante, / Todo es música y razón, / Y todo, como el diamante, / Antes que luz es carbón" ("All is beautiful and steadfast, / all is music and truth, / and all, like the diamond, / before becoming light, is coal") (163). The presence of Walt Whitman—democratic, human, all-embracing, fraternal—is undeniable in Martí, the creator of the notion of "our America." His three major collections of poetry are *Ismaelillo* (1882), which ushered in modernismo, according to many critics; *Versos sencillos* (1891); and the posthumous *Versos libres* (1913; "Free Verses"). Martí mastered all the lyrical registers, from fiery to tender, and was both social poet and in-gazing bard, the voice of both innocence and experience.

Presented here are "Sueño despierto" ("I Dream Awake"), an inner vision that allies the strength of elemental forces with childhood; "Musa traviesa" ("Naughty Muse"), which pays homage to fatherly love; and "Amor de ciudad grande" ("Love in the City"), which was written in New York in 1882 and is one of Martí's most accomplished works, a harbinger of modern poetry. Also included are "Si ves un monte de espumas . . ." ("If you see a mountain of ocean spray . . ."), an ars poetica; "Dos patrias" ("Two Countries"), a deceptively simple song of exile, a poem so fundamental in Latin American letters that Reinaldo Arenas would write his own version generations later (though about a very different Cuba); "Siempre que hundo la mente" ("Whenever I Plunge My Mind"), which augurs the new poetics; and "Contra el verso retórico" ("Against Rhetorical Poetry . . . "), a manifesto poem of natural, vertical, Icaran urges.

Martí was cut down during a guerrilla revolt, having been exiled numerous times—including, productively, to the United States. The precursor of *americanismo* would not live to see his dream, a Cuba free of Spanish rule, come true.

Sueño despierto

Yo sueño con los ojos
abiertos, y de día
y noche siempre sueño.
Y sobre las espumas
del ancho mar revuelto,
y por entre las crespas
arenas del desierto,
y del león pujante,
monarca de mi pecho,
montado alegremente,
sobre el sumiso cuello,
un niño que me llama
flotando siempre veo!

I Dream Awake

I dream with my eyes

open, and day

and night I'm forever dreaming.

On the spray

of the wide and stormy sea,

and through the rippling

desert sands,

atop the powerful lion,

monarch of my breast,

happily astride

his obedient neck,

a child there floating, calling to me

always do I see!

Musa traviesa

Mi musa? Es un diablillo

con alas de ángel.

¡Ah, musilla traviesa,

qué vuelo trae!

Yo suelo, caballero

en sueños graves,

cabalgar horas luengas

sobre los aires.

Me entro en nubes rosadas

bajo a hondos mares,

y en los senos eternos

hago viajes.

Allí asisto a la inmensa

boda inefable,

y en los talleres huelgo

de la luz madre:

Y con ella es la oscura

vida, radiante,

y a mis ojos los antros

son nidos de ángeles!

Al viajero del cielo,

¿qué el mundo frágil?

Pues ¿no saben los hombres

qué encargo traen?

¡Rasgarse el bravo pecho,

Naughty Muse

My muse? He's a little devil
with angel wings.
Oh, my naughty little muse,
how you can fly!

I, a horseman
in solemn dreams,
often ride the hours long
on the wind.
I plunge into roseate clouds
and plumb the oceans deep,
and in the eternal wombs
I journey.
There I attend the grand
ineffable wedding,
and in the workshops I am delighted
by mother light;
therewith dark life
turns radiant,
and caverns, to my eyes,
are the nests of angels!
To the rider in the sky,
how can the world be fragile?
For do men not know
what delivery they bring?
To tear open their fierce breast,

vaciar su sangre,
y andar, andar heridos,
muy largo valle,
roto el cuerpo en harapos,
los pies en carne,
hasta dar sonriendo
—¡No en tierra!—exánimes!
Y entonces sus talleres
la luz les abre,
y ven lo que yo veo:
¿Qué el mundo frágil?
Seres hay de montaña,
seres de valle,
y seres de pantanos
y lodazales.

De mis sueños desciendo,
volando vanse,
y en papel amarillo
cuento el viaje.
Contándolo, me inunda
un gozo grave:—
Y cual si el monte alegre,
queriendo holgarse,
al alba enamorando
con voces ágiles,
sus hilillos sonoros

to drain their blood,
and to walk, injured, on and on,
long, long is the valley across,
their ragged bodies broken,
feet turned raw
until smiling they come
upon—not land!—lifeless men!
And then light opens
their workshops,
and they see what I see:
How can the world be fragile?
There are creatures of the mountain,
creatures of the valley,
and creatures of
the mire and swamps.

I come down from my dreams,
they go flying off,
and on yellowed paper
I tell of the voyage.
I am overcome in the telling
by a weighty delight:—
and as if the joyful mountain,
wishing to take its pleasure,
winning the love of the dawn
with nimble cries,
its wispy threads of sound

desanudase,
y salpicando riscos,
labrando esmaltes,
refrescando sedientas
cálidas cauces,
echáralos risueños
por falda y valle,—
así, al alba del alma
regocijándose,
mi espíritu encendido
me echa a raudales
por las mejillas secas
lágrimas suaves.
Me siento, cual si en magno
templo oficiase;
cual si mi alma por mirra
vertiese al aire;
cual si en mi hombro surgieran
fuerzas de Atlante,
cual si el sol en mi seno
la luz fraguase:—
y estallo, hiervo, vibro,
alas me nacen!

untangling,

and sprinkling cliffs,

polishing the varnish of stones,

refreshing thirsty

hot riverbeds,

were gaily strewing sounds

over hill and dale—

so at the dawn of the soul

rejoicing,

my spirit afire

streams

gentle tears

down my dry cheeks;

I feel as if presiding

in a great temple;

as if bit by bit I were

shedding my soul into the air;

as if on my shoulders were emerging

the strength of Atlas,[1]

as if the light were forging

the sun in my breast:—

and I break out, seething, pulsing,

I am sprouting wings!

[1]Atlas was condemned to bear the heavens on his shoulders for his part in an uprising of Titans against Zeus.

Suavemente la puerta
del cuarto se abre,
y éntranse a él gozosos
luz, risas, aire.
Al par da el sol en mi alma
y en los cristales:
¡Por la puerta se ha entrado
mi diablo ángel!
¿Qué fue de aquellos sueños,
de mi viaje,
del papel amarillo,
de llanto suave?
Cual si de mariposas
tras gran combate,
volaran alas de oro
por tierra y aire,
así vuelan las hojas
do cuento el trance.
Hala acá el travesuelo
mi paño árabe;
allá monta en el lomo
de su incunable;
un carcax con mis plumas
fabrica y átase;
un sílex persiguiendo

Gently the door
to the room is opened,
and happily light and laughter,
air, come in.
While the sun shines down on my soul.
Through the door
and through the windowpanes has come:
my angelic devil!
What happened to my dreams,
my journey,
the yellowed paper,
my weeping softly?
As after some great battle,
the golden wings
of a butterfly
had flown over land and through the air,
so too fly the leaves of the book
where I tell of the trance.
The naughty little devil yanks
on my Arabian table cover;
He rides there on the spine
of his incunable;[2]
a quiver of my quills
he fashions and binds;
running after a paperweight

[2]An incunable is a book produced before 1501, from movable type.

vuelca un estante,
y ¡allá ruedan por tierra
versillos frágiles,
brumosos pensadores.
lópeos galanes!
De águilas diminutas
puéblase el aire:
¡Son las ideas, que ascienden,
rotas sus cárceles!

Del muro arranca, y cíñese,
indio plumaje:
aquella que me dieron
de oro brillante,
pluma, a marcar nacida
frentes infames,
de su caja de seda
saca, y la blande:
del sol a los requiebros
brilla el plumaje
que baña en áureas tintas
su audaz semblante.
De ambos lados el rubio
cabello al aire,
a mí súbito viénese

he upends a bookcase
and there go fragile little verses,
foggy thinkers,
Lopean young gents,[3]
tumbling to the floor!
The air is thronged
with tiny eagles:
Ideas! They are rising,
their prison cells smashed!

From the wall he pulls down
an Indian headdress and puts it on:
the dazzling gold one
I was given;
born to mark
villainous brows,
from its silken box
a quill he draws out and flourishes:
From sun and compliments
the feathers shine,
and bathe in aureate hues
his bold visage.
From both sides the blond
hair flying,
he comes running

---

[3]That is, in the manner of the Spanish Golden Age playwright Lope de Vega (1562–1635).

a que lo abrace.
De beso en beso escala
mi mesa frágil;
¡oh, Jacob, mariposa,
Ismaëlillo, ¡árabe!
¿Qué ha de haber que me guste
como mirarle
de entre polvo de libros
surgir radiante,
y, en vez de acero, verle
de pluma armarse,
y buscar en mis brazos
tregua al combate?
Venga, venga, Ismaelillo:
La mesa asalte,
y por los anchos pliegues
del paño árabe
en rota vergonzosa
mis libros lance,
y siéntese magnífico
sobre el desastre,
y muéstreme riendo,
Roto el encaje—

for an embrace.

Between my kisses he climbs

my fragile writing table;

O, Jacob,[4] butterfly,

Ismaelillo,[5] Arabian!

What will ever

please me more than seeing you

emerge radiant

from the midst of dusty books,

and instead of steel, to see you

take up arms with a quill,

and to seek in my arms

a truce to the fight?

Onward, onward, Ismaelillo:

attack the table,

and across the wide folds

of the Arabian cloth

cast my books

in shameful tatters,

and feel magnificent

over the disaster,

and let me see you laugh,

the lace having torn—

---

[4]The image of Jacob's ladder from Genesis 12 (the Hebrew *sullam* is actually "ramp" or "stairway") has been read as an allegory of the soul's progress heavenward or toward perfection.

[5]*Ismaelillo* is the diminutive of Ismael (Ishmael in English), which was also the name of Abraham's son in the Bible.

—¡Qué encaje no se rompe
en el combate!—
su cuello, en que la risa
gruesa onda hace!
¡Venga, y por cauce nuevo
mi vida lance,
y a mis manos la vieja
péñola arranque,
y del vaso manchado
la tinta vacíe!
¡Vaso puro de nácar:
Dame a que harte
esta sed de pureza:
Los labios cánsame!
¿Son éstas que lo envuelven
carnes, o nácares?
La risa, como en taza
de ónice árabe,
en su incólume seno
bulle triunfante:
¡Hete aquí, hueso pálido,
vivo y durable!
¡Hijo soy de mi hijo!
¡Él me rehace!

¡Pudiera yo, hijo mío,
quebrando el arte

What lace does not tear
in war!—
Your throat, where heavy waves
of laughter swell!
Come up here, and change the course
of my life,
pull from out my hands
the old quill,
and pour out the ink
from the tainted cup!
Pure nacre cup:
help me slake
this thirst for purity:
tire out these lips!
Be this flesh that envelops him,
or mother-of-pearl?
Laughter, as in a cup
of Arabian onyx,
in his unharmed breast
bubbles up triumphant:
Here it is, pale bone,
live and lasting!
I am the son of my son!
He remakes me!

If, my son,
by breaking with the way

universal muriendo,
mis años dándote,
envejecerte súbito,
La vida ahorrarte!—
Mas no: que no verías
en horas graves
entrar el sol al alma
y a los cristales!
Hierva en tu seno puro
risa sonante:
Rueden pliegues abajo
libros exangües:
Sube, Jacob alegre,
la escala suave:
Ven, y de beso en beso
mi mesa asaltes:—
¡Pues ésa es mi musilla,
mi diablo ángel!
¡Ah, musilla traviesa,
qué vuelo trae!

of the world, and dying,

giving you my years,

I could age you all at once,

to spare you life!—

But no: for you would not see

the sun come in the soul

and across the windowpanes

in solemn hours!

Let ringing laughter

bubble in your pure heart:

let bloodless books

tumble facedown to the floor:

Climb, merry Jacob,

the gentle ladder:

come, and between my kisses

attack my table:—

For this is my little muse,

my angelic devil!

Oh, naughty little muse,

how you can fly!

Amor de ciudad grande

De gorja son y rapidez los tiempos.
Corre cual luz la voz; en alta aguja
cual nave despeñada en sirte horrenda
húndese el rayo, y en ligera barca
el hombre, como alado, el aire hiende.
¡Así el amor, sin pompa ni misterio
muere, apenas nacido, de saciado!
Jaula es la villa de palomas muertas
y ávidos cazadores! Si los pechos
se rompen de los hombres, y las carnes
rotas por tierra ruedan, no han de verse
dentro más que frutillas estrujadas!

Se ama de pie, en las calles, entre el polvo
de los salones y las plazas: muere
la flor el día en que nace. Aquella virgen
trémula que antes a la muerte daba
la mano pura que a ignorado mozo;
el goce de temer; aquel salirse
del pecho el corazón; el inefable
placer de merecer; el grato susto
de caminar de prisa en derechura
del hogar de la amada, y a sus puertas
como un niño feliz romper en llanto;—
y aquel mirar, de nuestro amor al fuego,
irse tiñendo de color las rosas,—

Love in the City

Our age is one of gorge and haste.
The voice speeds like light; in the needle aloft
like a ship plunged into dire shoals,
lightning sinks, and in his swift craft,
man, as if wingèd, cleaves the air.
Thus does love, without pomp or mystery,
die spent, barely having lived.
The city is a cage of dead doves
and keen huntsmen! If men's hearts break
open, and their worn-out flesh
tumbles to the dust, you'll see nothing
but mashed-up berries inside!

One loves standing up, in the street, amidst the dust
of parlors and squares; the flower
dies the day it blooms. The trembling virgin
who once would sooner give her pure hand
to Death than to some strange boy;
the thrill of fearing: one's heart
leaping out of one's breast; the ineffable
pleasure of deserving; the pleasant fright
of hurrying on foot, making straight
for the beloved's house, then at her door,
to burst out crying like a happy child—
and our love's gaze into the fire,
the roses flushing with color—

¡ea, que son patrañas! Pues ¿quién tiene
tiempo de ser hidalgo? Bien que sienta
cual áureo vaso o lienzo suntuoso
dama gentil en casa de magnate!
O si se tiene sed, se alarga el brazo
ya a la copa que pasa, se la apura!
Luego, la copa turbia al polvo rueda,
y el hábil catador,—manchado el pecho
de una sangre invisible,—sigue alegre
coronado de mirtos, su camino!
No son los cuerpos ya sino desechos,
y fosas y jirones! Y las almas
no son como en el árbol fruta rica
en cuya blanda piel la almíbar dulce
en su sazón de madurez rebosa,—
sino fruta de plaza que a brutales
golpes el rudo labrador madura!

¡La edad es ésta de los labios secos!
De las noches sin sueño! De la vida
estrujada en agraz! Qué es lo que falta
que la ventura falta? Como liebre
azorada, el espíritu se esconde,
trémulo huyendo al cazador que ríe,
cual en soto selvoso, en nuestro pecho;

bah! A farce, all of it! Who has time
to be an aristocrat? Though the refined lady
in the magnate's house may feel
like an aureate cup or a lavish oil painting!
Or if one is thirsty, he reaches out
and drains the passing cup.
Then, the clouded cup falls to the dust,
and the skillful wine taster—his breast stained
with invisible blood—crowned with myrtle
goes merrily on his way!
No longer are they bodies, but the waste of men,
and graves and tatters! And their souls
are not like luscious fruit on the tree
in whose soft skin the sweet nectar
brims in its hour of ripeness—
but market-square fruit ripened
under the hard worker's brutal blows!

This is the age of dry lips!
Of sleepless nights! Of life
crushed into bitter grapes! What is missing
to gladden our hearts? Like a rattled hare,
the spirit hides away,
quivering, it eludes the laughing sportsman,
fleeing into our breast
as it would in the wilds of the forest;

y el deseo, de brazo de la fiebre,
cual rico cazador recorre el soto.

¡Me espanta la ciudad! ¡Toda está llena
de copas por vaciar, o huecas copas!
¡Tengo miedo ¡ay de mí! de que este vino
tósigo sea, y en mis venas luego
cual duende vengador los dientes clave!
¡Tengo sed,—mas de un vino que en la tierra
no se sabe beber! ¡No he padecido
bastante aún, para romper el muro
que me aparta ¡oh dolor! de mi viñedo!
Tomad vosotros, catadores ruines
de vinillos humanos, esos vasos
donde el jugo de lirio a grandes sorbos
sin compasión y sin temor se bebe!
Tomad! Yo soy honrado, y tengo miedo!

New York, abril 1882

and desire, arm in arm with fever,
like the wealthy huntsman prowls the woods.

The city horrifies me! It's all full
of cups waiting to be drained, and empty cups!
I'm afraid—dear God—that this wine
may be poison, and then, that it will clamp
its teeth into my veins like an avenging imp!
I thirst, but for a wine that cannot be
drunk on earth! I have not yet suffered
enough to tear down the wall
that keeps me—oh, the grief!—from my vineyard!
Vile wine tasters of a weak human vintage,
take the cups where you gulp down
the juice of the lily without compassion or fear!
Take them! I am honorable, and I am afraid!

New York, April 1882

Si ves un monte de espumas . . .

[*V, de Versos sencillos*]

Si ves un monte de espumas
es mi verso lo que ves:
Mi verso es un monte, y es
un abanico de plumas.

Mi verso es como un puñal
que por el puño echa flor:
Mi verso es un surtidor
que da un agua de coral.

Mi verso es de un verde claro
y de un carmín encendido:
Mi verso es un ciervo herido
que busca en el monte amparo.

Mi verso al valiente agrada:
Mi verso, breve y sincero,
es del vigor del acero
con que se funde la espada.

If you see a mountain of ocean spray . . .

[*V, from Simple Verses*]

If you see a mountain of ocean spray,
it is my poetry you see:
My poetry is a mountain,
and a fan made of feathers.

My poetry is like a knife,
flowering from the hilt:
My verse is a wellspring
whence coral waters rise.

My poetry is light green
and fiery crimson:
My poetry is a wounded stag
seeking shelter in the wild.

My poetry delights the brave:
my poetry, brief and genuine,
is as strong as the steel
with which the sword is fused.

Dos patrias

Dos patrias tengo yo: Cuba y la noche.
¿O son una las dos? No bien retira
su majestad el sol, con largos velos
y un clavel en la mano, silenciosa
Cuba cual viuda triste me aparece.
¡Yo sé cuál es ese clavel sangriento
que en la mano le tiembla! Está vacío
mi pecho, destrozado está y vacío
en donde estaba el corazón. Ya es hora
de empezar a morir. La noche es buena
para decir adiós. La luz estorba
y la palabra humana. El universo
habla mejor que el hombre.
                                        Cual bandera
que invita a batallar, la llama roja
de la vela flamea. Las ventanas
abro, ya estrecho en mí. Muda, rompiendo
las hojas del clavel, como una nube
que enturbia el cielo, Cuba, viuda, pasa . . .

Two Countries

I call two countries home: Cuba and the night.
Or are they both one? No sooner does the sun
draw back its majesty, than silent Cuba,
in long veils, a carnation in her hand,
appears to me like a grieving widow.
How well I know that bloody carnation
trembling in her hand! My breast
is empty, crushed, and empty
where once my heart used to be. Now the time has come
to begin to die. The night is a good time
to say good-bye. Light gets in the way,
and so too human speech. The universe
speaks better than man.

Like a flag

that is a call to war, the red flame
of the candle flutters. I open
windows, now closed off within myself. In silence,
tearing up the carnation petals, the widow Cuba
passes, like a cloud that leaves the heavens dark . . .

Siempre que hundo la mente

Siempre que hundo la mente en libros graves

la saco con un haz de luz de aurora:

Yo percibo los hilos, la juntura,

la flor del Universo: yo pronuncio

pronta a nacer una inmortal poesía.

No de dioses de altar ni libros viejos

no de flores de Grecia, repintadas

con menjurjes de moda, no con rastros

de rastros, no con lívidos despojos

se amasará de las edades muertas:

sino de las entrañas exploradas

del Universo, surgirá radiante

con la luz y las gracias de la vida.

Para vencer, combatirá primero:

E inundará de luz, como la aurora.—

Whenever I Plunge My Mind

Whenever I plunge my mind in solemn books,
I remove it with a beam of the light of dawn:
I perceive the threads, the seam,
the flower of the universe: I declare
an immortal poetry ready to be born.
Not one of gods on an altar or of old books,
not one of Greek flowers, repainted
with motley, modish hues, not with traces
of traces, not with pale remains
will it pile up from dead eras:
rather from the explored inner depths
of the universe will it emerge, shining
with the light and favor of life.
To overcome, first it shall fight:
And it will let loose a flood of light, like the dawn.—

Contra el verso retórico . . .

Contra el verso retórico y ornado
el verso natural. Acá un torrente:
Aquí una piedra seca. Allá un dorado
pájaro, que en las ramas verdes brilla,
como una marañuela entre esmeraldas.—
Acá la huella fétida y viscosa
de un gusano: los ojos, dos burbujas
de fango, pardo el vientre, craso, inmundo.
Por sobre el árbol, más arriba, sola
en el cielo de acero una segura
estrella; y a los pies el horno,
el horno a cuyo ardor la tierra cuece.
Llamas, llamas que luchan, con abiertos
huecos como ojos, lenguas como brazos,
savia como de hombre, punta aguda
cual de espada: la espada de la vida
que incendio a incendio gana al fin la tierra!
Trepa: viene de adentro: ruge: aborta.
Empieza el hombre en fuego y para en ala.

Y a su paso triunfal, los maculados,
los viles, los cobardes, los vencidos,
como serpientes, como gozques, como
cocodrilos de doble dentadura
de acá, de allá, del árbol que le ampara,
del suelo que le tiene, del arroyo

Against Rhetorical Poetry . . .

Against rhetorical and ornate verse,
natural poetry. Here a torrent:
There a dry stone. Away off, a golden
bird, gleaming in the green boughs,
like an Indian cress among emeralds.
Here the foul and slimy track
of a worm: its eyes, two bubbles of
mud, its underbelly brown, fat, and filthy.
High above the treetops
in the steely heavens, a lone
fixed star: down below, an oven,
by whose heat the earth is baking—
flames, battling flames, with open
holes for eyes, tongues for arms,
sap like human blood, razor tips
like those of a sword: the sword of life
that flame by flame shall gain the earth at last!
It climbs: it comes from within: it howls: it fails.
Man starts out in fire and ends up in wings.

As he passes, victorious, the disgraced,
the lowly, the cowards, the conquered,
like serpents, like whelps, like
crocodiles with two rows of teeth,
from all points, from the tree that gives him shelter,
from the ground that holds him, from the stream

donde apaga la sed, del yunque mismo
donde se forja el pan, le ladran y echan
el diente al pie, al rostro el polvo y lodo,
cuanto cegarle puede en su camino.
El, de un golpe de ala, barre el mundo
y sube por la atmósfera encendida
muerto como hombre y como sol sereno.
Así ha de ser la noble poesía:
Así como la vida: estrella y gozque;
la cueva dentellada por el fuego,
el pino en cuyas ramas olorosas
a la luz de la luna canta un nido,
canta un nido a la lumbre de la luna.

where he slakes his thirst, from the very anvil
where his bread is forged, they bark at him
and nip his feet, sling mud, and kick dust in his face,
all that can blind him on his path.
But with a single flap of his wings, he sweeps the world away
and rises on up through fiery space
dead as a man and as a peaceful sun.
Thus should noble poetry be:
And so too life: star and whelp;
a cave nibbled at by fire,
a pine tree in whose sweet-smelling branches
by the light of the moon a song comes forth from a nest,
a song comes forth from a nest in the moonlight.

Salvador Díaz Mirón

A man of pugnacious disposition, Díaz Mirón (1853–1928) became embroiled in several duels in the course of his life, the balance of which was the loss of the use of his left arm, the killing of two foes, and imprisonment on two occasions. The Mexican writer left one modernista masterpiece, *Lascas* ("Stone Chips") from 1901, a challenging collection of forty poems that he called his only authentic book. It opens with typical bravado in an ars poetica called "A mis versos" ("To My Poems"), which ends: "Id, las mías, deformes o bellas: / inspirad repugnancias o estimas, / Pero no sin dejar hondas huellas" ("Go forth [my rhymes], be you deformed or beautiful: / inspire repugnance or respect, / but not without leaving a deep impression") (399). Other important poems featured in it are "Epístola joco-seria" ("Seriocomic Epistle"), "Música de Schubert" ("Schubert's Music"), "Cintas de sol" ("Ribbons of Sun"),"Ecce Homo," "Nox," and "Gris de perla" ("Pearl Gray"). Díaz Mirón's best-known poem, "A Gloria" ("To Glory"), dates from his early period (1876–91), as does his Parnassian "Cleopatra." On the whole, he is most famous for his early work, mainly declamatory social protest poems of Romantic pedigree: "Víctor Hugo," "Sursum," "Voces Interiores" ("Inner Voices"), and the occasional rumination such as "Ojos verdes" ("Green Eyes").

Our selection here includes the erotic catalog "Cleopatra" and the uncharacteristically introverted "Música fúnebre" ("Funeral Music").

Works by Díaz Mirón probably first appeared in English in Samuel Beckett's translations in *Mexican Poetry: An Anthology*, compiled in 1958 by Octavio Paz (118–26).

Cleopatra

La vi tendida de espaldas
entre púrpura revuelta . . .
Estaba toda desnuda,
aspirando humo de esencias
en largo tubo, escarchado
de diamantes y de perlas.

Sobre la siniestra mano
apoyada la cabeza;
y como un ojo de tigre,
un ópalo daba en ella
vislumbres de fuego y sangre
el oro de su ancha trenza.

Tenía un pie sobre el otro,
y los dos como azucenas;
y cerca de los tobillos
argollas de finas piedras;
y en el vientre un denso triángulo
de rizada y rubia seda.

En un brazo se torcía,
como cinta de centella,
un áspid de filigrana
salpicado de turquesas,
con dos carbunclos por ojos
y un dardo de oro en la lengua.

Cleopatra

I saw her lying on her back
wrapped in purple . . .
She was naked, head to toe,
breathing in the smoke of essences
from a long frosted pipe
of diamonds and pearls.

On her left hand
rested her head;
and like a tiger's eye
an opal there
lent gleams of fire and blood
to her wide braid of gold.

One foot lay atop the other,
the pair like lilies;
and by her ankles,
rings of precious gems;
and at her womb, a thick triangle
of curly blond silk.

Up one arm twisting
like a ribbon of lightning,
an asp in ornamental arabesque
with turquoise flecked,
with two garnets for its eyes,
and its tongue a darting golden shaft.

A menudo suspiraba;
y sus altos pechos eran
cual blanca leche, cuajada
dentro de dos copas griegas,
y en alabastro vertida,
sólida ya, pero aun trémula.

¡Oh! yo hubiera dado entonces
todos mis lauros de Atenas,
por entrar en esa alcoba
coronado de violetas,
dejando con los eunucos
mis coturnos a la puerta.

Often would she sigh;
and her high, full breasts were
like white milk congealed
in two Greek goblets,
milk poured into alabaster,
now firm but quivering still.

Oh! I would have given
all my laurels from Athens
to go into that chamber
crowned with violets,
leaving my buskins
with the eunuchs
at the door.

Música fúnebre

Mi corazón percibe, sueña y presume.
Y como envuelta en oro tejido en gasa,
la tristeza de Verdi suspira y pasa
en la cadencia fina como un perfume.

Y frío de alta zona hiela y entume;
y luz de sol poniente colora y rasa;
y fe de gloria empírea pugna y fracasa,
como en ensayos torpes un ala implume.

El sublime concierto llena la casa;
y en medio de la sorda y estulta masa,
mi corazón percibe, sueña y presume.

Y como envuelta en oro tejido en gasa,
la tristeza de Verdi suspira y pasa
en la cadencia fina como un perfume.

Diciembre de 1899

Funeral Music

My heart senses, dreams, surmises.
As if shrouded in gold-embroidered crepe,
Verdi's sadness sighs and passes
in a cadence subtle as perfume.

And the highland cold chills and numbs;
and the setting sun's light colors and skims:
and faith in empyreal glory fights and fails,
like a featherless wing's clumsy stabs at flight!

The sublime concert fills the house;
and amidst the unhearing, stupid herd,
my heart senses, dreams, surmises.

And as if shrouded in gold-embroidered crepe,
Verdi's sadness sighs and passes
in a cadence subtle as perfume.

December 1899

Manuel Gutiérrez Nájera

An early modernista, Gutiérrez Nájera (1859–95) wrought masterpieces of musical, plastic, and chromatic skill that belie his reputation for producing mannered, *afrancesado* ("frenchified") verse. "Non omnis moriar" ("I Shall Not Die Altogether"), which engages Horace's ode (3.30), and "De blanco" ("In White"), with its studied Parnassian modeling of Théophile Gautier's synesthesic "Symphonie en blanc majeur," transcend mere imitation; the Mexican writer brought a genuine artistry, freedom, and love of beauty to his work. Moreover, his translations of Musset and Hugo were part of the output of a major, authentic poet, few though his collected poems may be. Excelling at journalism, poetry, and prose fiction, the Mexican wrote some landmark short stories: *Cuentos frágiles* (1883; "Fragile Tales") and *Cuentos color de humo* (1898; "Smoke-Colored Tales"). The second collection includes his often anthologized take on the Rip Van Winkle legend, "Rip-Rip." He founded Mexico's first modernista journal, the influential *Revista azul* ("Blue Review") in 1894. Important in his oeuvre are his essays against the positivistic encroachment on art—the imperative to produce utility. He argues in "El arte y el materialismo" ("Art and Materialism") for a freeing of the spiritual from the material, or rather for producing, above all, the beautiful, which he called "the representation of the infinite in the finite."

Gutiérrez Nájera would make major cultural contributions with his newspaper *crónicas* ("chronicles"), which he signed with dozens of pseudonyms: "Perico el de los Palotes" ("John Q. Public"); "Puck"; "Recamier"; and, most famously, "El Duque Job" ("Duke Job"), a name on which he played in his exhuberantly cosmopolitan poem "La duquesa Job" ("The Duchess Job"). As Cathy Jrade notes, the writer believed that art could be a force for redemption, shape history, and serve the national ends (36–39).

The despairing "To Be" washes over the reader with cataclysmic force; "Para entonces" ("When My Time Comes") depicts the theme of the *bel morir* ("beautiful death"); "Mis enlutadas" ("My Ladies in Mourning") may be read as a protopsychoanalytic fable.

To Be

¡Inmenso abismo es el dolor humano!
¿Quién vio jamás su tenebroso fondo?
Aplicad el oído a la abra oscura
de los pasados tiempos . . .
¡Dentro cae
lágrima eterna!
A las inermes bocas
que en otra edad movió la vida nuestra
acercaos curiosos . . .
¡Un gemido
sale temblando de los blancos huesos!
La vida es el dolor. Y es vida obscura,
pero vida también, la del sepulcro.
La materia disyecta se disuelve;
el espíritu eterno, la substancia,
no cesa de sufrir. En vano fuera
esgrimir el acero del suicida,
el suicidio es inútil! Cambia el modo,
el ser indestructible continúa!

¡En tí somos, Dolor, en tí vivimos!
La suprema ambición de cuanto existe
es perderse en la nada, aniquilarse,
dormir sin sueños . . .

To Be

A vast abyss is human pain!
Who has ever seen into its darkest depths?
Press your ear to the dark fissure
of bygone days . . .
Within it falls
an eternal teardrop!
To the helpless mouths
that our lives moved in days of old,
gather 'round, ye curious . . .
A moan
comes quaking out of the white bones!
Life is pain. And the life of the tomb
is no less life, though dark.
Dissected matter is undone;
the eternal spirit, the inner essence,
suffers without surcease. It would
be in vain to brandish the suicide's steel;
suicide is to no avail! The form changes,
the indestructible being lives on!

We exist in thee, Pain, in thee we live!
All things in creation yearn above all else
to disappear into nothingness, to be snuffed out,
to sleep an undreaming sleep . . .

¡Y la vida sigue
tras las heladas lindes de la tumba!
No hay muerte! En vano la llamáis a voces
almas sin esperanza! Proveedora
de seres que padezcan, la implacable
a otro mundo nos lleva. ¡No hay descanso!
Queremos reposar un solo instante
y una voz en la sombra dice: ¡Anda!
Sí ¡la vida es el mal! Pero la vida
no concluye jamás. El dios que crea,
es un esclavo de otro dios terrible
que se llama el Dolor. ¡Y no se harta
el inmortal Saturno! ¡Y el espacio,
el vivero de soles, lo infinito,
son la cárcel inmensa, sin salida,
de almas que sufren y morir no pueden!
¡Oh, Saturno inflexible, al fin acaba,
devora lo creado y rumia luego,
ya que inmortales somos, nuestras vidas!
Somos tuyos, Dolor, tuyos por siempre!
Mas perdona a los seres que no existen
sino en tu mente que estimula el hambre . . .
¡Perdón, oh Dios, perdón para la nada!
Sáciate ya. ¡Que la matriz eterna,
engendradora del linaje humano,
se torne estéril . . . que la vida pare . . .
¡Y ruede el mundo cual planeta muerto
por los mares sin olas del vacío!

And life goes on
beyond the icy confines of the tomb!
There is no death! In vain you call out for it,
all you souls bereft of hope! Progenitor
of suffering souls, the Implacable One
carries us off to the next life. There is no rest!
We hope for a single moment's respite
but a voice from the shadows commands: "Go forth!"
Yes, life is the malady! But life
is never-ending. The creator god
is the drudge of another terrible god
whose name is Pain. And immortal Saturn
is insatiable. And space,
the nursery of suns, the infinite reaches,
are the vast prison house with no escape
for souls that suffer and cannot die!
O, relentless Saturn, do away with created
things, devour them, and then,
since we are immortal, chew the cud of our lives!
We belong to thee, Pain, we are thine for time everlasting!
But have mercy on the creatures that do not exist
save in your mind that feeds on hunger . . .
Mercy, O God, have mercy on nothingness!
Have your fill at last. Let the eternal womb
that has sired the human generations
fall barren . . . Let life come to an end . . .
And let the world like a dead planet
wheel through the waveless seas of the void!

Para entonces

Quiero morir cuando decline el día,
en alta mar y con la cara al cielo;
donde parezca un sueño la agonía,
y el alma, un ave que remonta el vuelo.

No escuchar en los últimos instantes,
ya con el cielo y con la mar a solas,
más voces ni plegarias sollozantes
que el majestuoso tumbo de las olas.

Morir cuando la luz, triste, retira
sus áureas redes de la onda verde,
y ser como ese sol que lento expira:
algo muy luminoso que se pierde.

Morir, y joven; antes que destruya
el tiempo aleve la gentil corona;
cuando la vida dice aún: soy tuya,
aunque sepamos bien que nos traiciona!

When My Time Comes

I want to die when day is on the wane,
my face turned toward the sky, far out at sea;
where the throes of death seem but a dream,
and my soul, a bird that's taking to the sky.

Alone at last with the heavens and sea,
to hear no voice nor sobbing prayer
in my final moments
but the majestic roll and tumble of the waves.

To die when the dreary light hauls in
its golden nets from the sea-green waves,
and to be like the sun that burns out slow:
a shining light that's lost to view.

To die, and young; before faithless time
can break the courtly crown;
when life still says: I'm yours,
though well we know we'll be betrayed!

Mis enlutadas

Descienden taciturnas las tristezas
al fondo de mi alma,
y entumecidas, haraposas brujas,
con uñas negras
mi vida escarban.

De sangre es el color de sus pupilas,
de nieve son las lágrimas,
hondo pavor me infunden . . . ; yo las amo
por ser las solas
que me acompañan.

Aguárdolas ansioso, si el trabajo
de ellas me separa,
y búscolas en medio del bullicio,
y son constantes
y nunca tardan.

En las fiestas, a ratos se me pierden
o se ponen la máscara,
pero luego las hallo, y así dicen:
—¡Ven con nosotras!
¡Vamos a casa!

Suelen dejarme cuando sonriendo
mis pobres esperanzas

My Ladies in Mourning

Sorrows descend, melancholy,
        to the nethermost reaches of my soul;
paralytic, ragged hags
        are digging into my life, picking it clean
        with their black nails.

Blood is the color of their pupils,
        snow, the color of their tears;
they fill me with deep dread . . . ; I love them,
        for they are
        my only companions.

Anxiously I wait for them
        should their work keep us apart,
and search them out amidst the noise and haste;
        they are loyal,
        and never tarry long.

At parties sometimes I lose track of them
        or they don the mask,
but then I find them, whereupon they say:
        —Come with us!
        Let's go home!

Usually they leave me when
        my poor hopes,

como enfermitas ya convalecientes
salen alegres
a la ventana.

Corridas huyen, pero vuelven luego
y por la puerta falsa
entran trayendo como nuevo huésped
alguna triste,
lívida hermana.

Ábrese a recibirlas la infinita
tiniebla de mi alma,
y van prendiendo en ella mis recuerdos
cual tristes cirios
de cera pálida.

Entre esas luces, rígido tendido,
mi espíritu descansa;
y las tristezas, revolando en torno,
lentas salmodias,
rezan y cantan.

Escudriñando del húmedo aposento
rincones y covachas,
el escondrijo do guardé cuitado
todas mis culpas,
todas mis faltas.

like happy little convalescing patients,
    come out smiling
    to the window.

Chased off, they flee, but then come back
    in through the back door,
bringing a new guest,
    some mournful,
    ashen sister.

The infinite darkness of my soul
    parts to welcome them back,
and in it my memories are lit
    like somber tapers
    of pallid wax.

Encircled by the lights, laid out stiff,
    my spirit lies;
and my sorrows, fluttering hither and thither,
    pray and sing,
    intoning slow droning psalms.

Roving their gaze over the dank room,
    in corners and cubbyholes, the hiding place
where I, grieving, stored away
    all my sins,
    all my faults.

Y hurgando mudas, como hambrientas lobas,
las encuentran, las sacan,
y volviendo a mi lecho mortuorio
me las enseñan
y dicen: habla.

En lo profundo de mi ser bucean,
pescadoras de lágrimas,
y vuelven mudas con las negras conchas
en donde brillan
gotas heladas.

A veces me revuelvo contra ellas
y las muerdo con rabia,
como la niña desvalida y mártir
muerde a la harpía
que la maltrata.

Pero en seguida, viéndose impotente,
mi cólera se aplaca.
¿Qué culpa tienen, pobres hijas mías,
si yo las hice
con sangre y alma?

Venid, tristezas de pupila turbia,
venid, mis enlutadas,
las que viajáis por la infinita sombra,

And rummaging silently, like hungry she-wolves,
        they find them, rooting them out;
returning to my deathbed
        they show them to me
        and say: speak.

Deep down within me they plunge,
        diving for tears,
and come back, wordless, with black shells
        on which frozen droplets
        gleam.

At times I turn on them
        and bite them with rage,
like the helpless martyr girl
        bites the shrew
        who mistreats her.

But suddenly, finding itself powerless,
        my anger is appeased.
What fault is it of theirs, my poor daughters,
        for I made them
        out of my own blood and soul?

Come, my misty-eyed sorrows,
        come, my ladies in mourning,
you who range through the infinite shadows

donde está todo
lo que se ama.

Vosotras no engañáis: venid, tristezas,
¡oh mis criaturas blancas
abandonadas por la madre impía,
tan embustera,
por la esperanza!

Venid y habladme de las cosas idas,
de las tumbas que callan,
de muertos buenos y de ingratos vivos . . .
Voy con vosotras,
vamos a casa.

where lie
all things loved.

You won't deceive me: come, sorrows,
oh, my little white babies
abandoned by your ungodly mother,
by hope—
that filthy liar!

Come and speak to me of bygone things,
of the silent tombs,
of the noble dead and the ungrateful living . . .
I'm going with you,
let's go home.

Julián del Casal

Julián del Casal (1863–93) was one of the preeminent forerunners of modernismo, a hyperaesthetic poet who succumbed to fin-de-siècle neuroses, cosmopolitanism, exoticism—especially orientalism, and japonaiserie in particular—and frustrations sexual and religious. He was the archetypal tormented artist, one for whom life and art were coextensive. A dandy of the spirit, the young Cuban was literary kin to Poe, Mallarmé, Villiers de L'Isle-Adam, Jules Laforgue, Herrera y Reissig, and even Oscar Wilde. Casal's was the voluptuous realm of the "pálida pecadora" ("pale sinner"); death; half-revealed erotic truths; the sublime and "impuro amor" ("impure love") of the city (compare Martí's "Amor de ciudad grande" ["Love in the City"] with Casal's celebration of artifice in "En el campo" ["In the Country"]); nostalgia for the absent; transcendence through the ugly; sickness; and impossible beauty, which seemed to take a page from Jean Moréas's symbolist manifesto: "à vêtir l'Idée d'une forme sensible" ("to clothe the Idea in sensory form"). The writer turned away from Havana's provincialism and mercantilist values, felt mistrust and revulsion toward women, and obsessed over loss, ennui, and nothingness—almost to the point of nihilism. Always he kept his faith in the savior Art. Emilio de Armas saw in him a frustrated artist locked in battle not only with his surroundings but also with himself (41). To Casal, beauty was not escape but censure of the artless.

Two of his masterpieces, "Mis amores: Soneto Pompadour" ("My Loves: Pompadour Sonnet") and "Flores de éter" ("Flowers of Ether"), feature decadent catalogs of beauty—of the object and of the subject, respectively. In his "Neurosis," we find that peculiar admixture of world-weariness and longing so common in modernismo, often figured in princesses or courtesans. "En el campo" ("In the Country") sings of the triumph of the hothouse flower over those found in tedious nature.

Casal died young in a bloody bout of laughter after a consumptive, anguished life, leaving one of his heart's fondest desires—to see Paris—unfulfilled.

Mis amores

Soneto Pompadour

Amo el bronce, el cristal, las porcelanas,
las vidrieras de múltiples colores,
los tapices pintados de oro y flores
y las brillantes lunas venecianas.

Amo también las bellas castellanas,
la canción de los viejos trovadores,
los árabes corceles voladores,
las flébiles baladas alemanas,

el rico piano de marfil sonoro,
el sonido del cuerno en la espesura,
del pebetero la fragante esencia,

y el lecho de marfil, sándalo y oro,
en que deja la virgen hermosura
la ensangrentada flor de su inocencia.

My Loves

Pompadour Sonnet

I love bronze, crystal, porcelain,
stained glass windows of many hues,
tapestries painted with flowers and gold
and Venetian moons shining bright.

I love beautiful Castilian girls,
the song of the troubadours of old,
flying Arabian chargers,
woeful German ballads,

rich-toned pianos of echoing ivory,
the hunting horn's blast in the thicketed woods,
the fragrant essence of a swinging censer,

and the bed of ivory, sandalwood, and gold,
in which virgin beauty leaves
the bloody flower of its innocence.

Madame de Pompadour (1721–64) was mistress of Louis XV at Versailles. A courtly hairstyle was named for her.

Flores de éter

A la memoria de Luis II de Baviera

Rey solitario como la aurora,

rey misterioso como la nieve,

¿en qué mundo tu espíritu mora?

¿Sobre qué cimas sus alas mueve?

¿Vive con diosas en una estrella

como guerrero con sus cautivas,

o está en la tumba—blanca doncella

bajo coronas de siemprevivas? . . .

Aún eras niño, cuando sentías,

como legado de tus mayores,

esas tempranas melancolías

de los espíritus soñadores,

y huyendo lejos de los palacios

donde veías morir tu infancia,

te remontabas a los espacios

en que esparcíase la fragancia

de los ensueños que, hora tras hora,

Flowers of Ether

To the memory of Luis II of Bavaria

O solitary king as lone as dawn,

O mystery king as secret as the snow,

In what world does your spirit dwell?

In what mountain heights does it beat its wings?

Is it on a star with goddesses that it dwells

like a soldier with his women taken prisoner,

or is it in the tomb that it lies—pure maiden

wreathed in crowns of evergreen? . . .

You felt inside when still a child

passed down from elder kin

your precocious bouts of melancholy

to which dreamers of dreams are heir,

and far from palaces you fled

from where you saw your childhood fade,

and back you harked to places then

where lingered scents of reveries strewn,

daydreams that with every passing hour

Ludwig Friedrich Wilhelm (1845–86), king of Bavaria, was an eccentric, archromantic ruler known variously as "mad King Ludwig," "the dream king," and "the swan king." A fanatical devotee of Richard Wagner and patron of the arts, Ludwig suffered a loss of mental faculties that closely followed the composer's death. The ruler died by drowning—some say of his own accord, having long struggled to repress his homosexuality. See McIntosh; and Visconti's film portrait *Ludwig*.

minando fueron tu vida breve,
rey solitario como la aurora,
rey misterioso como la nieve.

Si así tu alma gozar quería
y a otras regiones arrebatarte,
un bajel tuvo: la Fantasía;
Y un mar espléndido: el mar del Arte.
¡Cómo veías sobre sus ondas
temblar las luces de nuevos astros
que te guiaban a las Golcondas
donde no hallabas del hombre rastros;
y allí sintiendo raros deleites
tu alma encontraba deliquios santos,
como en los tintes de los afeites
las cortesanas frescos encantos!
Por eso mi alma la tuya adora
y recordándola se conmueve,
rey solitario como la aurora,
rey misterioso como la nieve.

Colas abiertas de pavos reales,
róseos flamencos en la arboleda,
fríos crepúsculos matinales,

would gnaw your fleeting life away,
O solitary king as lone as dawn,
O mystery king as secret as the snow.

If thus your soul was minded to enjoy
and to other regions spirit you away,
one craft: the ship of Fantasy it had;
and too a splendid sea: the sea of Art.
From over whitecap peaks you'd spy
the quivering lights of heavenly new spheres
that set your course Golconda's way,[1]
where no trace of man you found;
and there, feeling odd and rarefied delights,
your soul swooned with sacred decadence
akin to courtesans who find new charms
in cosmetics' colorations!
Wherefore my soul does worship yours
which moves me when it's called to mind,
O solitary king as lone as dawn,
O mystery king as secret as the snow.

Tails of peacocks fanned out full,
flamingos pink in woodland grove,
the daybreaks' morning chill,

---

[1]Golconda, a ruined city in India celebrated once for its vast diamond production, now proverbially connotes a place of tremendous wealth.

áureos dragones en roja seda,
verdes luciérnagas en las lilas,
plumas de cisnes alabastrinos
sonidos vagos de las esquilas,
sobre hombros blancos encajes finos,
vapor de lago dormido en calma,
mirtos fragantes, nupciales tules,
nada más bello fue que tu alma
hecha de vagas nieblas azules
y que a la mía sólo enamora
de las del siglo décimo nueve,
rey solitario como la aurora,
rey misterioso como la nieve.

Aunque sentiste sobre tu cuna
caer los dones de la existencia,
tú no gozaste de dicha alguna
más que en los brazos de la Demencia.
Halo llevabas de poesía
y más que el brillo de tu corona
a los extraños les atraía
lo misterioso de tu persona
que apasionaba nobles mancebos,
porque ostentabas en formas bellas
la gallardía de los efebos
con el recato de las doncellas.

golden dragons, silky red,
fireflies green that dart in lilac glade,
white plumage of the alabaster swans,
faint-sounding cowbell's clang,
white shoulders draped in finest lace,
the lake-locked steam in slumber's still,
myrtles fragrant, wedding tulles,
nothing was more beautiful than your soul,
wrought of misty azure haze,
and mine falls in love with none
but nineteenth-century souls,
O solitary king as lone as dawn,
O mystery king as secret as the snow.

Though in your cradle you could sense
the shower of life's gifts,
no bliss at all was yours
but Insanity's embrace.
A halo of poetry did you wear
and more than for the splendor of your aureole,
drawn strangers would unite
around your mystery persona,
which held the noble adolescent boys in thrall,
for you displayed in beautiful ways
a young man's gallant arts combined
with a modest maiden's charms.

Tedio profundo de la existencia,
sed de lo extraño que nos tortura,
de viejas razas mortal herencia,
de realidades afrenta impura,
visión sangrienta de la neurosis,
delicuescencia de las pasiones,
entre fulgores de apoteosis
tu alma llevaron a otras regiones
donde gloriosa ciérnese ahora
y eterna dicha sobre ella llueve,
rey solitario como la aurora,
rey misterioso como la nieve.

The tedium profound of life,
the torture of our thirsting for the strange,
fey legacy from ancient peoples passed,
impure affront to reality,
a bloody vision of neurosis,
the passions in a deliquescent brew,
amid apotheosis flashes
your soul was to other regions rapt
where it hovers now, to glory gone,
and eternal joy rains down upon it,
O solitary king as lone as dawn,
O mystery king as secret as the snow.

Neurosis

Noemí, la pálida pecadora
de los cabellos color de aurora
y las pupilas de verde mar,
entre cojines de raso lila,
con el espíritu de Dalila,
deshoja el cáliz de un azahar.

Arde a sus plantas la chimenea
donde la leña chisporrotea
lanzando en torno seco rumor,
y alzada tiene su tapa el piano
en que vagaba su blanca mano
cual mariposa de flor en flor.

Un biombo rojo de seda china
abre sus hojas en una esquina
con grullas de oro volando en cruz,
y en curva mesa de fina laca
ardiente lámpara se destaca
de la que surge rosada luz.

Blanco abanico y azul sombrilla,
con unos guantes de cabritilla
yacen encima del canapé,
mientras en taza de porcelana,
hecha con tintes de la mañana,
humea el alma verde del té.

Neurosis

Naomi, the pale sinner
with the dawn-colored tresses
and the sea-green eyes,
on lilac-colored satin cushions,
with the heart of Delilah
strips away the calyx from an orange blossom.

At her heels burns the hearth fire
where the firewood sparks and crackles,
sending dull sounds flying;
the piano lid is raised,
her white hand wanders over the keys
as a butterfly flits from flower to flower.

A red folding screen of Chinese silk
opens its leaves in a corner
with a cross-shaped flock of gold cranes winging,
and on an artful varnished writing table
a burning lamp stands out,
shining its roseate light.

White fan and blue parasol,
kid gloves lie on the settee,
while in a porcelain cup
made in hues of morning,
the green soul of the tea sits steaming.

Pero ¿qué piensa la hermosa dama?
¿Es que su príncipe ya no la ama
como en los días de amor feliz,
o que en los cofres del gabinete
ya no conserva ningún billete
de los que obtuvo por un desliz?

¿Es que la rinde cruel anemia?
¿Es que en sus búcaros de Bohemia
rayos de luna quiere encerrar,
o que, con suave mano de seda,
del blanco cisne que amaba Leda
ansía las plumas acariciar?

¡Ay! es que en horas de desvarío
para consuelo del regio hastío
que en su alma esparce quietud mortal,
un sueño antiguo le ha aconsejado
beber en copa de ónix labrado
la roja sangre de un tigre real.

But what is the beautiful lady thinking?
Could it be her prince no longer loves her
as in days of happy love gone by?
Or that in the coffers in her dresser drawer
she has not a single love letter left
from those an affair had brought her?

Could cruel anemia be what overcomes her?
Could it be she wishes to trap moonbeams
in her Bohemian vases,
or that with smooth silken hand
she yearns to stroke the plumage
of the white swan whom Leda loved?

Alas! In hours of delirium
in solace for the queenly weariness
which through her soul spreads deadly stillness,
an ancient dream has counseled her
to drink from a carved onyx goblet
the red blood of a royal tiger.

En el campo

Tengo el impuro amor de las ciudades,
y a este sol que ilumina las edades
prefiero yo del gas las claridades.

A mis sentidos lánguidos arroba,
más que el olor de un bosque de caoba,
el ambiente enfermizo de una alcoba.

Mucho más que las selvas tropicales,
plácenme los sombríos arrabales
que encierran las vetustas capitales.

A la flor que se abre en el sendero,
como si fuese terrenal lucero,
olvido por la flor de invernadero.

Más que la voz del pájaro en la cima
de un árbol todo en flor, a mi alma anima
la música armoniosa de una rima.

Nunca a mi corazón tanto enamora
el rostro virginal de una pastora
como un rostro de regia pecadora.

In the Country

I have the impure love of cities,
and as for this sun that illuminates the ages
I would rather have the gaslight's glow.

My languid senses are entranced
less by the smell of a mahogany woods
than by a bedroom's sickly air.

Much more than tropical jungles,
I am fond of the gloomy slums
that the ancient capitals contain.

The flower that opens along the lane,
as if it were an earthbound Venus shining,
I leave behind for the hothouse flower.

More than the birdsong atop a tree
all aflower, my soul is moved
by the harmonic music of a rhyme.

Never can my heart be stolen
so much by the virgin visage of a shepherd girl
as by the queenly sinner's face.

Al oro de las mies en primavera,
yo siempre en mi capricho prefiriera
el oro de teñida cabellera.

No cambiara sedosas muselinas
por los velos de nítidas neblinas
que la mañana prende en las colinas.

Más que al raudal que baja de la cumbre,
quiero oír a la humana muchedumbre
gimiendo en su perpetua servidumbre.

El rocío que brilla en la montaña
no ha podido decir a mi alma extraña
lo que el llanto al bañar una pestaña.

Y el fulgor de los astros rutilantes
no trueco por los vívidos cambiantes
del ópalo, la perla o los diamantes.

To the ripe and golden fields of spring
I forever in my fancies would prefer
the gold of tresses dyed.

I would not trade silken muslins
for the veils of bright mist
the morning hangs in the hills.

More than the torrent that flows down from the heights,
I wish to hear the human throng
moaning in their lifelong servitude.

The dew that sparkles in the hills
has failed to say to my strange soul
what tears can tell as they bathe a lash.

And the shine of twinkling stars
I would not trade for the vivid iridescence
of opal, pearl, or diamond.

José Asunción Silva

The short and tortured life of José Asunción Silva (1865–96) was full of heartbreaks and literary turns. A case in point: in 1895, the steamship *Amérique*, on which he was traveling, wrecked, and with it were lost the Colombian's reputedly greatest works. These included many poems and a compendium of the crises of the fin de siècle, the novel *De sobremesa (After-Dinner Conversation)*, which he reconstructed shortly before his death. With his financial situation perilous (as it almost always was), he visited his doctor friend Juan Evangelista Manrique, whom he famously asked to draw the exact outline on his chest of where the human heart is located. Early on 24 May 1896, he shot himself through the heart with a rusty revolver.

Silva's "Nocturno III" ("Nocturne III"), one of the best-known poems in the Spanish language, is still memorized and recited. Excerpts of it are even printed on the back of the 5000-peso note in Colombia. The poem's tragic protagonists are *sombras* (Spanish for "shadows" or "shades," the second term connoting spirits in the underworld). In "Ars" ("Ars Poetica"), we see the conceit of poetry as the alchemical quintessence. "Vejeces" ("Things Past"), with its echoes of Charles Baudelaire's "Spleen (2)" (from *Flowers of Evil*) and Gustavo Adolfo Bécquer's Rima VII ("Del salón en el ángulo oscuro . . ." ["There in the dark corner of the room . . ."]), asserts the esthetic of the antique. "El mal del siglo" ("*Mal du Siècle*") describes a typically ambivalent view of a member of the rationalist order. "Melancolía" ("Melancholia") captures the nostalgia for unity, a fin de siècle preoccupation.

Indebted to Poe, Heine, Hugo, and Bécquer, Silva's poetry—essentially symbolist—is full of suggestion and polyrythmic innovation. His poetry bears witness to the reality behind the appearance, the enduring amid the ephemeral, the spiritual over the corporeal, and the music in the chaos. Yet Silva's poetic universe is largely a crepuscular one, in which all the philosophically pessimistic modes run riot: despair, anomie, morbidity, separateness, emptiness, abulia. One of his distraught narrators even interrogates the stars for their sphinx-like incommunication: "Por qué os calláis si estáis vivas / y por qué alumbrais si estáis muertas?" ("Why do you stay silent if you are alive / and why do you give light if you are dead?") ("Estrellas").

Silva's work attracts growing numbers of devotees around the world.

Nocturno III

Una noche

una noche toda llena de perfumes, de murmullos y de músicas de älas,

una noche

en que ardían en la sombra nupcial y húmeda, las luciérnagas fantásticas,

a mi lado, lentamente, contra mí ceñida, toda,

muda y pálida

como si un presentimiento de amarguras infinitas,

hasta el fondo más secreto de tus fibras te agitara,

por la senda que atraviesa la llanura florecida

caminabas,

y la luna llena

por los cielos azulosos, infinitos y profundos esparcía su luz blanca,

y tu sombra

fina y lángida

y mi sombra

por los rayos de la luna proyectada

sobre las arenas tristes

de la senda se juntaban

y eran una

y eran una

¡y eran una sola sombra larga!

¡Y eran una sola sombra larga!

¡Y eran una sola sombra larga!

Nocturne III

One night
one night full of perfumes, whispers, music of wings,
one night
in which fantastic fireflies burned in the humid nuptial gloom,
slowly, pressing closely at my side, and wholly,
hushed and pallid
as if foretasting bitternesses measureless,
to your most secret depths it shook you, every fibre of your frame,
down the lane through the budding plain
you walked,
and the full moon
through endless heavens blue-imbued and deep was strewing its
white light,
and your slender,
languid shadow
and my shadow
by moonbeams cast
on mournful sands
of the lane, were joined together.
And they were one
and they were one
they were one long single shadow!
They were one long single shadow!
They were one long single shadow!

Esta noche
solo, el alma
llena de las infinitas amarguras y agonías de tu muerte,
separado de ti misma, por la sombra, por el tiempo y la distancia,
por el infinito negro,
donde nuestra voz no alcanza,
solo y mudo
por la senda caminaba,
y se oían los ladridos de los perros a la luna,
a la luna pálida
y el chillido
de las ranas,
sentí frío, era el frío que tenían en la alcoba
tus mejillas y tus sienes y tus manos adoradas,
¡entre las blancuras níveas
de las mortüorias sábanas!
Era el frío del sepulcro, era el frío de la muerte,
Era el frío de la nada . . .
Y mi sombra
por los rayos de la luna proyectada,
iba sola,
iba sola
¡iba sola por la estepa solitaria!
Y tu sombra esbelta y ágil
fina y lánguida,
como en esa noche tibia de la muerta primavera,

Tonight,

alone, my soul

filled with bitternesses measureless, the endless torment of your death,

torn from you in body, by darkness, time and distance,

by boundless black,

beyond where our voice can travel,

alone and hushed

along the lane I went walking,

and the baying of dogs at the moon could be heard,

at the pale moon

and the croaking

of frogs,

I felt a chill, the chill that was upon your cheeks,

your temples, your hands beloved, in your chamber

under your shroud's

snowy white folds!

It was the tomb's cold chill, it was the chill of death,

it was the chill of nothingness . . .

And my shadow

by moonbeams cast,

walked on alone,

walked on alone,

walked on alone along the solitary plain!

And your nimble, slender shadow,

slight and languid,

like that warm night in dead of spring,

como en esa noche llena de perfumes, de murmullos y de músicas
de alas,
se acercó y marchó con ella,
se acercó y marchó con ella,
se acercó y marchó con ella . . . ¡Oh las sombras enlazadas!
¡Oh las sombras que se buscan y se juntan en las noches de negruras
y de lágrimas! . . .

as on that night full of perfumes, whispers, and the music of wings,
drew in close and it walked with mine,
drew in close and it walked with mine,
drew in close and it walked with mine . . . Oh, two shadows
interlaced! Oh,
shadows that seek each other out and join as one in blackest nights,
in nights of tears! . . .

Ars

El verso es un vaso santo. Poned en él tan sólo,
un pensamiento puro,
en cuyo fondo bullan hirvientes las imágenes
como burbujas de oro de un viejo vino oscuro!

Allí verted las flores que en la continua lucha
ajó del mundo el frío,
recuerdos deliciosos de tiempos que no vuelven,
y nardos empapados de gotas de rocío

Para que la existencia mísera se embalsame
cual de una esencia ignota
quemándose en el fuego del alma enternecida
de aquel supremo bálsamo basta una sola gota!

Ars Poetica

Poetry is a sacred chalice. Place in it
pure thought alone,
whose images seething boil in its bottom
like the golden bubbles of an old dark wine!

Cast into it the faded flowers that a cold world
has withered with its ceaseless strife.
Memories sweet of times that are no more,
and spikenards drenched in dew.

For this wretched existence to be perfumed,
salved as in some essence unknown,
burning in the fire of the loving Soul,
one needs of this supreme balsam but a single drop!

Vejeces

Las cosas viejas, tristes, desteñidas,
sin voz y sin color, saben secretos
de las épocas muertas, de las vidas
que ya nadie conserva en la memoria,
y a veces a los hombres, cuando inquietos
las miran y las palpan, con extrañas
voces de agonizante dicen, paso,
casi al oído, alguna rara historia
que tiene oscuridad de telarañas,
són de laúd, y suavidad de raso.

¡Colores de anticuada miniatura,
hoy, de algún mueble en el cajón, dormida;
cincelado puñal; carta borrosa,
tabla en que se deshace la pintura
por el tiempo y el polvo ennegrecida;
histórico blasón, donde se pierde
la divisa latina, presuntuosa,
medio borrada por el liquen verde;
misales de las viejas sacristías;
de otros siglos fantásticos espejos
que en el azogue de las lunas frías
guardáis de lo pasado los reflejos;
arca, en un tiempo de ducados llena,
crucifijo que tanto moribundo,

Things Past

Old, sad, faded things,
colorless and voiceless, know secrets
from dead eras, from the lives
no one still preserves in their memory.
Sometimes men, when restless,
will look at them, and touch them, and
with the strange voices of the dying, they tell softly,
almost in one's ear, some peculiar tale,
cobweb-dark and satin-smooth,
with the sweet strains of a lute.

The colors of an antique miniature
now slumbering in a drawer;
a chiseled knife; a shadowy letter;
a canvas from which the paint is peeling down
from age and dust blackened;
a historic coat of arms, where
the vainglorious Latin motto is fading,
nearly effaced by green lichen;
missals from old sacristies;
you, phantasmal mirrors from other centuries
that in the quicksilver of cold moons
store reflections of things past;
chest, once full of ducats;
crucifix that so many at death's door

humedeció con lágrimas de pena
y besó con amor grave y profundo;
negro sillón de Córdoba; alacena
que guardaba un tesoro peregrino
y donde anida la polilla sola;
sortija que adornaste el dedo fino
de algún hidalgo de espadín y gola;
mayúsculas del viejo pergamino;
batista tenue que a vainilla hueles;
seda que te deshaces en la trama
confusa de los ricos brocateles;
arpa olvidada que al sonar, te quejas;
barrotes que formáis un monograma
incomprensible en las antiguas rejas,
el vulgo os huye, el soñador os ama
y en vuestra muda sociedad reclama
las confidencias de las cosas viejas!
El pasado perfuma los ensueños
con esencias fantásticas y añejas
y nos lleva a lugares halagüeños
en épocas distantes y mejores,
por eso a los poetas soñadores,
les son dulces, gratísimas y caras,
las crónicas, historias y consejas,
las formas, los estilos, los colores
las sugestiones místicas y raras
y los perfumes de las cosas viejas!

bathed with tears of grief
and kissed with a profound and solemn love;
old black Cordovan armchair; wardrobe
that held a traveled treasure
and where the moth makes her nest alone;
you, ring, that graced the slender finger
of some sword-and-ruff nobleman;
the illuminated initials of an old manuscript;
you flimsy cambric, redolent of vanilla;
silk, you come undone in the jumbled
skein of the rich brocatelles;
forgotten harp, you groan when plucked;
crosspieces, you spell an indecipherable monogram
in the ancient grillwork—
the masses shun you all, the dreamer loves you,
and in your silent company recovers
the secrets that old things confide!
The past perfumes one's reveries
with whimsical, time-ripened essences
and transports us to alluring places
in far-off eras better than our own,
wherefore the dreaming poets find
chronicles, histories, and legends,
forms, styles, and colors,
impressions mystical and strange
and the perfumes of old things
to be charming, sweet, and dear!

El mal del siglo

El paciente

Doctor, un desaliento de la vida
que en lo íntimo de mí se arraiga y nace,
el mal del siglo . . . el mismo mal de Werther,
de Rolla, de Manfredo y de Leopardi.
Un cansancio de todo, un absoluto
desprecio por lo humano . . . un incesante
renegar de lo vil de la existencia
digno de mi maestro Schopenhauer;
un malestar profundo que se aumenta
con todas las torturas del análisis . . .

El médico

Eso es cuestión de régimen; camine
de mañanita; duerma largo, báñese;
beba bien; coma bien; cuídese mucho,
¡lo que usted tiene es hambre!

Mal du Siècle

PATIENT

Doctor, a loss of heart to live

in my innermost being is taking root and growing,

the *mal du siècle* . . . the same ill that Werther,

Rolla, Manfred, and Leopardi suffered.[1]

A weariness of it all, an absolute

disdain for things human . . . an incessant

disowning of the meanness of existence

worthy of my master Schopenhauer;[2]

a profound malaise that worsens

with all the tortures of analysis . . .

DOCTOR

That's a matter of regime; walk

at daybreak; sleep long, bathe;

drink well; eat well; take good care,

what you have is hunger!

---

[1]Werther is the archromantic young suicide in *The Sorrows of Young Werther* (1774), by Goethe (1749–1832). Rolla is a skeptical character in "Rolla" (1833), by Alfred de Musset (1810–57). Manfred is the outcast hero of an 1817 poem of the same name by Byron (1788–1824). Giacomo Leopardi (1798–1837) was a despairing Italian lyric poet.

[2]Arthur Schopenhauer (1788–1860) was a post-Kantian solipsist and pessimist who denounced the illusory desires that feed the perpetual pain of life. He wrote *The World as Will and Idea* (1818).

Melancolía

De todo lo velado,
tenue, lejana y misteriosa surge
vaga melancolía
que del ideal al cielo nos conduce.

He mirado reflejos de ese cielo
en la brillante lumbre
con que ahuyenta las sombras, la mirada
de sus ojos azules.

Leve cadena de oro
que una alma a otra alma con sus hilos une
oculta simpatía,
que en lo profundo de lo ignoto bulle,

y que en las realidades de la vida
se pierde y se consume
cual se pierde una gota de rocío
sobre las yierbas que el sepulcro cubren.

Melancholia

From all things veiled,

tenuous, mysterious, remote,

a vague melancholy looms

to lead us from the ideal to heaven.

I have seen reflections of that heaven

in the brilliant glow

with which the gaze of her blue eyes

puts the shadows to flight.

Airy chain of gold

which unseen sympathy,

seething in the depths of the unknown,

links soul to soul with its filaments

and that in the concrete forms of life

is lost and swallowed up

as a dewdrop is lost

in the blades of grass that overlie the tomb.

Rubén Darío

The figure most closely associated with modernismo, Rubén Darío (1867–1916) was an aristocrat of the spirit even as his real life succumbed to dissipation and bohemianism. The Nicaraguan is one of the great moderns, transcending his Parnassian and symbolist roots—as he writes, "No hay escuelas; hay poetas" (137; "There are no schools; there are poets")—and embodying many of modernismo's principles and even contradictions. With equal genius his production embraces vatic evocations of lost pagan worlds; proud pan-Hispanic assertions of hispanidad; poignant confessions from the eternal battle of flesh and spirit; and consolatory, programmatic apotheoses of art and the artist that also reprehended the growing insensitivity and intranscendence of the philistine classes. Harmony could be said to be Darío's muse—to capture the graceful action, the measured rhythm, the insightful correspondence. Darío innovated new forms, renewed old ones (the sonnet, the ballad), and opened new possibilities with the musicality, flexibility, and vigor he brought to poetry in Spanish. His three most influential works are *Azul* (1888; "Azure"), *Prosas profanas y otros poemas* (1896; "'Profane Hymns' and Other Poems"), and *Cantos de vida y esperanza* (1905; "Songs of Life and Hope"). A journalist, diplomat, and cultural critic, he joined his historical moment to cosmic time, modernity to the ages.

Here we feature "El cisne" ("The Swan"), one of several of Darío's classical treatments of the emblematic bird; "El reino interior" ("The Kingdom Within"), a long parabolic reverie; "Yo persigo una forma . . ." ("I Seek a Form . . ."), which dramatizes his and his contemporaries' verbal quest; "La página blanca" ("The Blank Page"), a poem that employs tropes beloved of the modernistas—exotic travel and dream visions; "A Roosevelt" ("To Roosevelt"), a political work written in response to Theodore Roosevelt's gunboat diplomacy; "¡Torres de Dios! ¡Poetas! . . . " ("Towers of God! Poets! . . . "), a celebration of the autonomy of art; "¡Carne, celeste carne de la mujer . . . !" ("Flesh, Heavenly Flesh of Woman . . . !"), an apotheosis of woman; and "En las constelaciones" ("In the Constellations"), a poem that represents both artists' fascination at the time with Pythagorean thought and Darío's own conflicting impulses.

El cisne

Fue en una hora divina para el género humano.
El cisne antes sólo cantaba para morir.
Cuando se oyó el acento del Cisne wagneriano
fue en medio de una aurora, fue para revivir.

Sobre las tempestades del humano oceano
se oye el canto del Cisne; no se cesa de oír,
dominando el martillo del viejo Thor germano
o las trompas que cantan la espada de Argantir.

¡Oh Cisne! ¡Oh sacro pájaro! Si antes la blanca Helena
del huevo azul de Leda brotó de gracia llena,
siendo de la Hermosura la princesa inmortal,

bajo tus blancas alas la nueva Poesía
concibe en una gloria de luz y de armonía
la Helena eterna y pura que encarna el ideal.

The Swan

It happened in a divine hour for the human race.

The swan, before, had only sung to die.

When the voice of the Wagnerian swan was heard,[1]

it was amidst a dawning day, he sang to live again.

Over the storming sea of humanity

the song of the Swan is heard; it is heard without end,

overpowering the hammer of old Germanic Thor

and the trumpets singing of the sword of Argantyr.[2]

O Swan! O holy bird! If before, Leda's blue egg

brought forth white Helen full of grace,[3]

the immortal princess of Beauty,

under your white wings the new Poetry

conceives in a heaven of harmony and light

the pure, eternal Helen who embodies the ideal.

French Symbolism

---

[1]Reference is to the opera *Lohengrin*, by Richard Wagner (1813–83), which recounts the legend of the knight of the swan, as he was known.

[2]Argantyr is the hero of the Icelandic myth *Hyndluljoth*.

[3]In Greek myth, Leda is mother of Helen of Troy, in legend the most beautiful woman of antiquity; Clytemnestra; and Castor and Pollux. In later versions, the swan (Zeus in disguise) fathered Leda's children. See William Butler Yeats's "Leda and the Swan," which depicts the mating as an act of violence.

El reino interior

A Eugenio de Castro.

. . . With Psychis, my Soul!
—Poe

Una selva suntuosa

en el azul celeste su rudo perfil calca.

Un camino. La tierra es de color de rosa,

cual la que pinta fra Doménico Cavalca

en sus Vidas de santos. Se ven extrañas flores

de la flora gloriosa de los cuentos azules,

y entre las ramas encantadas, papemores

cuyo canto extasiara de amor a los bulbules.

(*Papemor*: ave rara; *Bulbules*: ruiseñores.)

Mi alma frágil se asoma a la ventana obscura

de la torre terrible en que ha treinta años sueña.

La gentil Primavera, primavera le augura.

La vida le sonríe rosada y halagüeña.

Y ella exclama: «¡Oh fragante día! ¡Oh sublime día!

Se diría que el mundo está en flor; se diría

que el corazón sagrado de la tierra se mueve

con un ritmo de dicha; luz brota, gracia llueve.

The Kingdom Within

To Eugenio de Castro

. . . with Psyche, my Soul.
—*Poe*

A sumptuous jungle
traces its rugged profile against the blue sky.
A pathway. The earth is rose-colored,
like the one Father Dominic Cavalca depicts
in his lives of the saints.[1] Strange flowers are seen,
the glorious flora from out of the nursery tales,
and midst the enchanted boughs, the papemors'
song sends the philomels into loving raptures.
(*Papemor*: rare bird; *philomels*: nightingales.)

My delicate soul looks out the dark window
of the terrible tower in which lo these thirty years she's dreamed.
Graceful Spring casts her an augury of spring.
Rose-colored life, full of promise, smiles upon my soul;
she cries: "Oh sweet-smelling day! Oh day sublime!
It is as if the world is on the bloom; it is as if
the sacred heart of the earth moves
to a joyous beat; light sprouts up and grace rains down.

The epigraph is from Edgar Allan Poe's "Ulalume." Darío writes "Psychis" for "Psyche." In classical mythology, Psyche was loved by Eros (Cupid) and was the personification of the soul.

[1]Cavalca (c. 1270–1342), an Italian preacher and Dominican, was the translator of *Lives of the Fathers* and other exempla.

¡Yo soy la prisionera que sonríe y que canta!»

Y las manos liliales agita, como infanta
real en los balcones del palacio paterno.

¿Qué són se escucha, són lejano, vago y tierno?
Por el lado derecho del camino adelanta
el paso leve una adorable teoría
virginal. Siete blancas doncellas, semejantes
a siete blancas rosas de gracia y de harmonía
que el alba constelara de perlas y diamantes.
¡Alabastros celestes habitados por astros:
Dios se refleja en esos dulces alabastros!
Sus vestes son tejidos del lino de la luna.
Van descalzas. Se mira que posan el pie breve
sobre el rosado suelo, como una flor de nieve.
Y los cuellos se inclinan, imperiales, en una
manera que lo excelso pregona de su origen.
Como al compás de un verso, su suave paso rigen.
Tal el divino Sandro dejara en sus figuras
esos graciosos gestos en esas líneas puras.
Como a un velado són de liras y laúdes,
divinamente blancas y castas pasan esas
siete bellas princesas. Y esas bellas princesas
son las siete Virtudes.

I am the imprisoned maiden who smiles and sings!"

And her lily-white hands she waves, like a crown

princess on the balcony of her father's palace.

What sweet strains are heard afar, sounds dreamy, soft and tender?

On the right side of the pathway

a charmed processional of virgins quickens its unhurried gait.

Seven white maidens like

seven white roses of grace and harmony

that the dawn has inlaid with diamond and pearl constellations.

Heaven-blue alabasters inhabited by stars:

God is reflected in those honeyed alabasters!

Their raiments are woven of moon flax.

They are bare of foot. One sees their wispy feet alight

on the rosy ground like a snow flower.

Their imperial necks bend so

that their sublimity of mien proclaims to all their noble caste.

To the rhythms of a verse they bid their gentle steps.

In such pure lines might the divine Botticelli[2]

have rendered his figures' graceful movements.

As if to a sweet secret sound of lyres and lutes,

the seven fair princesses, divinely white and

chaste, pass by. And these beauties

are the seven Virtues.

---

[2]The early Renaissance painter Botticelli (1445–1510) is known especially for *Birth of Venus* (c. 1485) and *Primavera* (1477–78).

Al lado izquierdo del camino y paralela-
mente, siete mancebos—oro, seda, escarlata,
armas ricas de Oriente—hermosos, parecidos
a los satanes verlenianos de Ecbatana,
vienen también. Sus labios sensuales y encendidos,
de efebos criminales, son cual rosas sangrientas;
sus puñales, de piedras preciosas revestidos
—ojos de víboras de luces fascinantes—,
al cinto penden; arden las púrpuras violentas
en los jubones; ciñen las cabezas triunfantes
oro y rosas; sus ojos, ya lánguidos, ya ardientes,
son dos carbunclos mágicos del fulgor sibilino,
y en sus manos de ambiguos príncipes decadentes
relucen como gemas las uñas de oro fino.
Bellamente infernales,
llenan el aire de hechiceros veneficios
esos siete mancebos. Y son los siete Vicios,
los siete poderosos Pecados capitales.

Y los siete mancebos a las siete doncellas
lanzan vivas miradas de amor. Las Tentaciones.
De sus liras melifluas arrancan vagos sones.
Las princesas prosiguen, adorables visiones
en su blancura de palomas y de estrellas.

To the left of the pathway and side by
side, seven youths—gold, silk, and scarlet,
luxurious weapons from the Orient—beautiful, looking like
the Verlainean Satans of Ecbatana,[3]
make their way as well. Their sensual lips afire,
the lips of murderous ephebes, are like bloody roses;
their knives, encrusted with precious stones
—snake eyes with bewitching gleams,
hang from their waists; the violent purples of their doublets
blaze; gold and roses gird their exultant brows;
their eyes, by turns languid, then of flame,
are two magic carbuncles of sibylline splendor,
and in their hands, the hands of an ambiguous, decadent prince,
their fine golden nails shine like gems.
Beautifully infernal,
the seven adolescents
fill the air with veneficial charms.[4] And they are the seven Vices,
the mighty seven deadly Sins.

And the seven young men to the seven maidens
cast deep loving looks their way. Temptations.
From their honey-flowing lyres they draw faint sounds.
The princesses carry on, charmed visions
in their whiteness of doves, their whiteness of stars.

---

[3]The poem "Crimen Amoris," by Paul Verlaine (1844–96), features "beautiful demons, adolescent Satans brave" who "[t]o the seven sins their fivefold senses gave" (223; trans. Clark Ashton Smith).

[4]*Veneficial*: acting by poison; used in poisoning or in sorcery (obsolete).

Unos y otras se pierden por la vía de rosa,
y el alma mía queda pensativa a su paso.
—«¡Oh! ¿Qué hay en ti, alma mía?
¡Oh! ¿Qué hay en ti, mi pobre infanta misteriosa?
¿Acaso piensas en la blanca teoría?
¿Acaso
los brillantes mancebos te atraen, mariposa?»

Ella no me responde.
Pensativa se aleja de la obscura ventana
—pensativa y risueña,
de la Bella-durmiente-del-Bosque tierna hermana—
y se adormece en donde
hace treinta años sueña.

Y en sueño dice: «¡Oh dulces delicias de los cielos!
¡Oh tierra sonrosada que acarició mis ojos!
—¡Princesas, envolvedme con vuestros blancos velos!
        —¡Príncipes, estrechadme con vuestros brazos rojos!»

Man and maid are lost to view on the rosy path,
and my soul is lost in thought as they pass.
"Oh! What's got into you, my soul?
Oh! What's got into you, my poor mysterious infanta?
Are you thinking perchance of the white processional?
Could you be
attracted by the dazzling young men, my butterfly?"

She makes no reply.
In thought she draws back from the dark window
—thoughtful, smiling,
the gentle sister of the Sleeping Beauty of the wood—
and slumbers where
she has dreamt these thirty years.

And in dreams she says: "Oh sweet delights of heaven!
Oh rose-colored earth that caressed my eyes!
Princesses, enclose me in your white veils!
        Princes, embrace me tight in your red arms!"

Yo persigo una forma . . .

Yo persigo una forma que no encuentra mi estilo,
botón de pensamiento que busca ser la rosa;
se anuncia con un beso que en mis labios se posa
al abrazo imposible de la Venus de Milo.

Adornan verdes palmas el blanco peristilo;
los astros me han predicho la visión de la Diosa;
y en mi alma reposa la luz, como reposa
el ave de la luna sobre un lago tranquilo.

Y no hallo sino la palabra que huye,
la iniciación melódica que de la flauta fluye
y la barca del sueño que en el espacio boga;

y bajo la ventana de mi Bella-Durmiente,
el sollozo continuo del chorro de la fuente
y el cuello del gran cisne blanco que me interroga.

I Seek a Form . . .

I seek a form that my style cannot find,
a bud of thought that seeks to be a rose;
it is augured by a kiss that alights on my lips
in the impossible embrace of the Venus de Milo.

Green palm leaves grace the white colonnade;
the stars foretold to me the vision of the Goddess;
and illumination settles on my soul
as the moonbird reposes on a placid lake.

And naught do I discover but the word that flees,
the melodious initiation that flows from the flute,
the ship of dreams set sailing through all space,

and under the window of my Sleeping Beauty,
the sobbing, sobbing of the waters of the fountain,
and the neck of the great white swan, that questions me.

French Symbolism

La página blanca

A A. Lamberti

> *Mis ojos miraban en hora de ensueños*
> *la página blanca.*

Y vino el desfile de ensueños y sombras.

Y fueron mujeres de rostros de estatua,

mujeres de rostros de estatuas de mármol,

¡tan tristes, tan dulces, tan suaves, tan pálidas!

Y fueron visiones de extraños poemas,

de extraños poemas de besos y lágrimas,

¡de historias que dejan en crueles instantes

las testas viriles cubiertas de canas!

¡Qué cascos de nieve que pone la suerte!

¡Qué arrugas precoces cincela en la cara!

¡Y cómo se quiere que vayan ligeros

los tardos camellos de la caravana!

Los tardos camellos

—como las figuras en un panorama—,

cual si fuese un desierto de hielo,

atraviesan la página blanca.

Éste lleva

una carga

de dolores y angustias antiguas,

angustias de pueblos, dolores de razas;

The Blank Page

For A. Lamberti

In time of reverie, my eyes gazed
at the blank page.

And the parade of reveries and shadows came.

And they were statue-faced women,

women with the faces of marble statues,

so sad, so sweet, so gentle, so pale!

And they were visions of poems never seen before,

wondrous poems of kisses and of tears,

of stories that in a cruel flash turn

manly heads of hair to gray!

Such snowy helmets are our lot!

What wrinkles fate carves in our face before our time!

And how one hopes that the caravan's lagging camels

step lively with the lightest loads!

The lagging camels

—like figures in a panoramic scene,

as if from a desert wilderness of ice—

move across the blank page.

This one bears

a burden

of ancient pains and grief,

the grief of nations, the pains of races;

¡dolores y angustias que sufren los Cristos
que vienen al mundo de víctimas trágicas!

Otro lleva
en la espalda
el cofre de ensueños, de perlas y oro,
que conduce la reina de Saba.

Otro lleva
una caja
en que va, dolorosa difunta,
como un muerto lirio, la pobre Esperanza.

Y camina sobre un dromedario
la Pálida,
la vestida de ropas obscuras,
la Reina invencible, la bella inviolada:

la Muerte.
¡Y el hombre,
a quien duras visiones asaltan,
el que encuentra en los astros del cielo
prodigios que abruman y signos que espantan,

mira al dromedario
de la caravana
como al mensajero que la luz conduce,
en el vago desierto que forma
la página blanca!

the pains and grief endured by the Christs
who come to this world of tragic victims!

Another bears
on its back
the chest of reverie, pearls, and gold;
this beast the Queen of Sheba drives.

Another bears
a box
transporting the sorrowful departed:
poor Hope lies like a lily, dead.

On camelback comes riding
the Bloodless One,
she of the dark raiment,
the invincible Queen, the inviolate beauty:

Death.
And man,
assailed by cruel visions,
finding in the stars up in the heavens
astounding wonders and terrifying signs,

gazes at the dromedary
in the caravan
as if at a messenger guided by the light,
on the hazy desert that is
the blank page!

A Roosevelt

¡Es con voz de la Biblia, o verso de Walt Whitman,
que habría que llegar hasta ti, Cazador!
¡Primitivo y moderno, sencillo y complicado,
con un algo de Washington y cuatro de Nemrod!

Eres los Estados Unidos,
eres el futuro invasor
de la América ingenua que tiene sangre indígena,
que aun reza a Jesucristo y aun habla en español.

Eres soberbio y fuerte ejemplar de tu raza;
eres culto, eres hábil; te opones a Tolstoy.
Y domando caballos, o asesinando tigres,
eres un Alejandro-Nabucodonosor.
(Eres un profesor de Energía,
como dicen los locos de hoy.)

Crees que la vida es incendio,
que el progreso es erupción,

To Roosevelt

One could reach you, Hunter,

with the voice of the Bible, or the poetry of Walt Whitman.

Primitive and modern, simple and complicated,

one part George Washington and four parts Nimrod.[1]

You are the United States,

you are the future invader

of the naive America with its indigenous blood, the America

that still prays to Jesus and still speaks Spanish.

You are a proud, strong exemplar of your race;

you are learned, you are skilled; you stand against Tolstoy.

Breaking horses or killing tigers,

you are an Alexander-Nebuchadnezzar.[2]

(You are a master of energy,

as the madmen say nowadays.)[3]

You think life is a fire,

that progress is an outbreak;

---

[1]Nimrod was a biblical king, "a mighty hunter before the Lord" (Gen. 10.9 [King James Vers.]).

[2]The Russian novelist Leo Tolstoy (1828–1910) was noted for his simplicity and nonviolence. Alexander the Great (356–323 BCE) was a legendary conqueror. Nebuchadnezzar was a king and great builder in ancient Babylonia (605–562 BCE).

[3]Reference is to Theodore Roosevelt's cult of activity expounded in his book *The Strenuous Life* (1900) (Zárate 205n17).

que en donde pones la bala
el porvenir pones.
No.

Los Estados Unidos son potentes y grandes.
Cuando ellos se estremecen hay un hondo temblor
que pasa por las vértebras enormes de los Andes.
Si clamáis, se oye como el rugir del león.
Ya Hugo a Grant lo dijo: «Las estrellas son vuestras.»
(Apenas brilla, alzándose, el argentino sol
y la estrella chilena se levanta . . .) Sois ricos.
Juntáis al culto de Hércules el culto de Mammón;
y alumbrando el camino de la fácil conquista,
la Libertad levanta su antorcha en Nueva-York.

Mas la América nuestra, que tenía poetas
desde los viejos tiempos de Netzahualcoyotl,
que ha guardado las huellas de los pies del gran Baco,
que el alfabeto pánico en un tiempo aprendió;
que consultó los astros, que conoció la Atlántida,
cuyo nombre nos llega resonando en Platón,
que desde los remotos momentos de su vida
vive de luz, de fuego, de perfume, de amor,

wherever your bullet flies,

there the future strikes.

No.

The United States is powerful and great.

When it trembles, a tremor runs

deep down the giant spine of the Andes.

Your cry sounds like the lion's roar.

As Hugo said to Grant: "The stars are yours."

(The Argentinean sun has only just risen,

and Chile's star is on the rise . . .) You are rich.

You wed the cult of Hercules to the cult of Mammon.[4]

And lighting the way to easy conquest,

Lady Liberty holds her torch aloft in New York.

But our America, which has had poets

from the ancient times of Nezahualcóyotl,[5]

and has preserved the footsteps of the great Bacchus,

who at a single stroke learned Pan's alphabet;[6]

our America, which consulted the stars, which knew Atlantis,

whose name comes ringing down the ages through Plato,

and which, from the earliest moments of its life,

has lived on light, on fire, on perfume, and on love;

---

[4]In the New Testament, Mammon was the false god of worldly gain or materialism.

[5]Philosopher-king (1402–72) of what is today Texcoco, Mexico.

[6]Bacchus (Dionysis) is the god of wine, Pan (Faunus) the god of nature and sexuality.

la América del grande Moctezuma, del Inca,
la América fragante de Cristobal Colón,
la América católica, la América española,
la América en que dijo el noble Guatemoc:
«Yo no estoy en un lecho de rosas»; esa América
que tiembla de huracanes y que vive de Amor;
hombres de ojos sajones y alma bárbara, vive.
Y sueña. Y ama, y vibra; y es la hija del Sol.
Tened cuidado. ¡Vive la América española!
Hay mil cachorros sueltos del León Español.
Se necesitaría, Roosevelt, ser, por Dios mismo,
el Riflero terrible y el fuerte Cazador,
para poder tenernos en vuestras férreas garras.

Y, pues contáis con todo, falta una cosa: ¡Dios!

the America of the great Montezuma, of the Inca,
the fragrant America of Columbus,
Catholic America, Spanish America,
the America in which noble Cuauhtemoc asked:
"Am I then upon a bed of roses?"[7] The America
trembling in hurricanes and living on Love.
O you men of Anglo-Saxon eyes and barbarian souls: this America lives.
And dreams. And loves, and pulses; for she is the daughter of the Sun.
Watch out. Spanish America is alive!
A thousand cubs born of the Spanish Lion are on the loose.
Roosevelt, you would have to have God Himself on your side
to be the fearsome Rifleman, the mighty Hunter,
to catch us in your iron clutches.

And though all is yours, one thing you lack is—God!

[7]Cuauhtemoc (1502–25), last Aztec emperor, was defeated and tortured by the Spaniards. The quote here is taken from Alan Seeger's poem "The Torture of Cuauhtemoc."

¡Torres de Dios! ¡Poetas! . . .

¡Torres de Dios! ¡Poetas!
¡Pararrayos celestes
que resistís las duras tempestades,
como crestas escuetas,
como picos agrestes,
rompeolas de las eternidades!

La mágica esperanza anuncia un día
en que sobre la roca de armonía
expirará la pérfida sirena.
¡Esperad, esperemos todavía!

Esperad todavía.
El bestial elemento se solaza
en el odio a la sacra poesía
y se arroja baldón de raza a raza.
La insurrección de abajo
tiende a los Excelentes.
El caníbal codicia su tasajo
con roja encía y afilados dientes.

Torres, poned al pabellón sonrisa.
Poned, ante ese mal y ese recelo,
una soberbia insinuación de brisa
y una tranquilidad de mar y cielo . . .

Towers of God! Poets! . . .

Towers of God! Poets!
Heavenly lightning rods
that weather harsh storms
like unprotected crests,
like wild summits,
breakwaters of eternity!

Magical Hope foretells a day
when on the rock of harmony
the treacherous siren will perish.
Hold out hope, let us keep hope alive!

Keep hope alive.
The brutish sort find solace
in their hatred of sacred poetry,
and abuse is heaped from race to race.
The uprising from below
takes aim at the Nobles.
The cannibal covets his hunk of salted meat
with red gums and sharpened teeth.

Towers, fly your colors with a smile.
And against that ill and distrust,
a proud hint of a breeze
and the calm of sea and sky . . .

¡Carne, celeste carne de la mujer . . . !

¡Carne, celeste carne de la mujer! Arcilla
—dijo Hugo—; ambrosía más bien, ¡oh maravilla!
La vida se soporta,
tan doliente y tan corta,
solamente por eso:
roce, mordisco o beso
en ese pan divino
para el cual nuestra sangre es nuestro vino.
En ella está la lira,
en ella está la rosa,
en ella está la ciencia armoniosa,
en ella se respira
el perfume vital de toda cosa.

Eva y Cipris concentran el misterio
del corazón del mundo.
Cuando el áureo Pegaso
en la victoria matinal se lanza
con el mágico ritmo de su paso
hacia la vida y hacia la esperanza,
si alza la crin y las narices hincha
y sobre las montañas pone el casco sonoro
y hacia la mar relincha,
y el espacio se llena

Flesh, Heavenly Flesh of Woman . . . !

Flesh, heavenly flesh of woman! Clay,
wrote Hugo; ambrosia, rather. O thing of wonder!
It alone makes life,
so painful and so short,
endurable:
a caress, a nibble or a kiss
of that divine bread
for which our blood is our wine.
In it lies the lyre,
in it lies the rose,
in it lies harmonious knowledge,
in it the life-giving essence
of all things is breathed.

Eve and Cypris[1] alone embody the mystery
of the heart of the world.
When golden Pegasus
in morning's victory breaks
toward life and hope
in the magic rhythm of his gait,
his mane flying, nostrils flared,
and over hills he rides with hooves resounding,
whinnying toward the sea,
and space all fills

---

[1]Cypris is better known as Aphrodite, Greek goddess of love, beauty, and sexual desire.

de un gran temblor de oro,
es que ha visto desnuda a Anadiomena.

Gloria, ¡oh Potente a quien las sombras temen!
¡Que las más blancas tórtolas te inmolen,
pues por ti la floresta está en el polen
y el pensamiento en el sagrado semen!

Gloria, ¡oh Sublime, que eres la existencia
por quien siempre hay futuros en el útero eterno!
¡Tu boca sabe al fruto del árbol de la Ciencia
y al torcer tus cabellos apagaste el infierno!

Inútil es el grito de la legión cobarde
del interés, inútil el progreso
yankee, si te desdeña.
Si el progreso es de fuego, por ti arde.
¡Toda lucha del hombre va a tu beso,
por ti se combate o se sueña!

Pues en ti existe Primavera para el triste,
labor gozosa para el fuerte,
néctar, Ánfora, dulzura amable.
¡Porque en ti existe
el placer de vivir, hasta la muerte
ante la eternidad de lo probable . . . !

with a great golden quake,
it is because he has seen Anadyomene[2] naked.

O Mighty Glory, feared by shadows!
For the whitest turtledoves offer you in sacrifice,
for your sake the woods are in pollen
and thought is in sacred semen!

O Sublime Glory, you are existence
for whom there are forever futures in the eternal womb!
Your mouth tastes of the fruit from the Tree of Knowledge
and by wringing out your hair you quenched the fires of Hell!

In vain is the cry of the cowardly legion
of the selfish; in vain, Yankee
progress, if it shuns you.
If progress is of fire, it burns for you.
All man's strife is bound for your kiss,
for you one fights and dreams!

For in you there is Spring for the heavy-hearted,
joyful work for the strong,
nectar, amphorae, and tender kindness.
For in you resides
the joy of living unto death
faced with the eternity of what, chances are, will be . . . !

---

[2]Another epithet for Aphrodite, after Apelles's painting *Aphrodite Rising from the Sea* (*anadyomene* in Greek means "rising").

En las constelaciones

En las constelaciones Pitágoras leía,

yo en las constelaciones pitagóricas leo;

pero se han confundido dentro del alma mía

el alma de Pitágoras con el alma de Orfeo.

Sé que soy, desde el tiempo del Paraíso, reo;

sé que he robado el fuego y robé la armonía;

que es abismo mi alma y huracán mi deseo;

que sorbo el infinito y quiero todavía . . .

Pero ¿qué voy a hacer, si estoy atado al potro

en que, ganado el premio, siempre quiero ser otro,

y en que, dos en mí mismo, triunfa uno de los dos?

En la arena me enseña la tortuga de oro

hacia dónde conduce de las musas el coro

y en dónde triunfa, augusta, la voluntad de Dios.

In the Constellations

In the constellations Pythagoras would read,
I read in the Pythagorean constellations;
but within my soul, Pythagoras's soul
has fused with the soul of Orpheus.

I know that since the days of Eden, a captive I have been;
I know that I have stolen fire and harmony;
that my soul is an abyss and a hurricane is my desire;
that I gulp down the infinite and still I thirst . . .

But what can I do? For I am bound to the torture rack
on which, my laurels won, I always wish to be another,
and that I am two in one, and one of the two shall rule.

In the sand the golden tortoise traces
the way for me to where the choir of muses leads
and to the time when God's majestic will prevails.

Ricardo Jaimes Freyre

The title of the first collection of the Bolivian poet Ricardo Jaimes Freyre (1868–1933) was *Castalia bárbara* (1899; "Pagan Spring"), an echo of Leconte de Lisle's *Poèmes barbares* (1854). It paid homage to the Norse mythological tradition, notably in its Wagnerian overtures and interludes in the manner of grand opera: "Crespas olas adheridas a las crines / de los ásperos corceles de los vientos; / alumbradas por rojizos resplandores, / cuando en yunque de montañas su martillo bate el trueno" ("Angry waves clinging to the manes / of the hard chargers of the winds; / lit by reddish flashes / when on the mountain's anvil the thunderclap his hammer pounds") ("Camino"). The poet looks to a mysterious past, often medieval, even to mythologize his own heroic voice: "¿En / qué lid, en qué claustros, en qué castillo / espada, cruz o lira tuve en mi mano . . . ?" ("In what battle, in what cloisters, in what castle / did I hold sword, cross, or lyre in hand . . . ?") ("Antepasados"). Leopoldo Lugones wrote in his introduction to Jaimes Freyre's first book that his is an "impersonal e interno" ("Prólogo" xiii; "impersonal and inward") poetry pregnant with unexpected communication with the inanimate, and wrought of "nostalgia, de quimera y de ensueño (xi; "nostalgia, chimeras and reverie").

"Æternum vale" ("Farewell Forever") dramatizes the twilight of the gods. "El canto del mal" ("The Song of Evil") evokes another figure from mythology, the ambiguous trickster-demon Loki. "Las voces tristes" ("The Doleful Cries") conjures a Scandinavian or Icelandic inner landscape ("sobre el vasto desierto / flota una vaga sensación de angustia" ["over the vast wasteland / floats a dim feeling of anguish"]); "Lo fugaz" ("Ephemera"), from *Los sueños son vida* (1917; "Dreams Are Life"), is a meditation on the body-soul problem.

Æternum vale

Un Dios misterioso y extraño visita la selva.
Es un Dios silencioso que tiene los brazos abiertos.
Cuando la hija de Thor espoleaba su negro caballo,
le vio erguirse, de pronto, a la sombra de un añoso fresno.
Y sintió que se helaba su sangre
ante el Dios silencioso que tiene los brazos abiertos.

De la fuente de Imér, en los bordes sagrados, más tarde,
la Noche a los Dioses absortos reveló el secreto;
el Aguila negra y los Cuervos de Odín escuchaban,
y los Cisnes que esperan la hora del canto postrero;
y a los Dioses mordía el espanto
de ese Dios silencioso que tiene los brazos abiertos.

En la selva agitada se oían extrañas salmodias;
mecía la encina y el cauce quejumbroso viento;
el bisonte y el alce rompían las ramas espesas,
y a través de las ramas espesas huían mugiendo.
En la lengua sagrada de Orga
despertaban del canto divino los divinos versos.

Æternum vale ("Farewell Forever")

A strange mysterious God has come to the woods.
He is a silent God with open arms.
While the daughter of Thor[1] spurred her black steed on,
she saw Him rise up suddenly in the shadow of an ancient ash tree.
And she felt her blood run cold
before the silent God with open arms.

Later, the Gods listening rapt at the sacred boundary,
Night revealed the secret of Mimir's well;[2]
the black Eagle and the Crows of Odin were listening in,
and the Swans that await their death song's hour;
and fright gnawed away at the Gods,
terror of that silent God with open arms.

From the woods all aflutter came strange droning songs;
a moaning wind swayed the evergreen oak and the willow;
the buffalo and the elk were snapping thick branches,
and through the thick branches they ran away bellowing.
In the sacred tongue of Orcus[3]
the divine verses of the consecrated song were stirring from their sleep.

---

[1]Thrud, whose name means "power," was the daughter of Thor and one of the Valkyries.

[2]In Norse mythology, the well of the highest wisdom is Meomresburna (Mímisbrunar), named for Mimir (also Mimer or Meomer), the giant who guards its prophetic water. It is located under the roots of Yggdrasil, the world tree, whose three roots stretch into the underworld, Hel; the world of the frost giants; and the world of human beings.

[3]Orcus is the abode of the dead, the underworld.

Thor, el rudo, terrible guerrero que blande la maza
—en sus manos es arma la negra montaña del hierro—
va a aplastar, en la selva, a la sombra del árbol sagrado,
a ese Dios silencioso que tiene los brazos abiertos.
Y los dioses contemplan la maza rugiente,
que gira en los aires y nubla la lumbre del cielo.
. . . .
Ya en la selva sagrada no se oyen las viejas salmodias
ni la voz amorosa de Freya cantando a lo lejos;
agonizan los dioses que pueblan la selva sagrada
y en la lengua de Orga se extinguen los divinos versos.

Solo, erguido a la sombra de un árbol,
hay un Dios silencioso que tiene los brazos abiertos.

Warlike Thor, coarse and awe-inspiring, brandishing his hammer
—the black mountain of steel is a weapon in his hands—
goes off to the shadow of the sacred tree in the wood,
to crush the silent God with open arms.
And the Gods look on at the roaring war club,
whirling in the wind and clouding over the light from the sky.

. . . .

And in the sacred wood the old chants have fallen silent,
no longer is Freya's tender voice heard singing in the distance;
the Gods that inhabit the sacred wood are dying,
and in Orcus's tongue the verses of the Gods are flickering out.

Alone, risen in the shadow of a tree,
a silent God stands with open arms.

El canto del mal

Canta Lok en la oscura región desolada,
y hay vapores de sangre en el canto de Lok.
El Pastor apacienta su enorme rebaño de hielo,
que obedece—gigantes que tiemblan—la voz del Pastor.
Canta Lok a los vientos helados que pasan,
y hay vapores de sangre en el canto de Lok.

Densa bruma se cierne. Las olas se rompen
en las rocas abruptas, con sordo fragor.
En su dorso sombrío se mece la barca salvaje
del guerrero de rojos cabellos, huraño y feroz.
Canta Lok a las olas rugientes que pasan,
y hay vapores de sangre en el canto de Lok.

Cuando el himno del hierro se eleva al espacio
y a sus ecos responde siniestro clamor,
y en el foso, sagrado y profundo, la víctima busca,
con sus rígidos brazos tendidos, la sombra del Dios,
canta Lok a la pálida Muerte que pasa
y hay vapores de sangre en el canto de Lok.

The Song of Evil

In the dark desolate region Loki sings,[1]

and whiffs of blood exhale from Loki's song.

The Shepherd grazes his vast flock of ice,

which—trembling giants—heeds the Shepherd's voice.

Loki sings to the frozen, passing winds,

and whiffs of blood exhale from Loki's song.

A thick fog hangs overhead. Waves break

against the steep rocks with a dull roar.

On their somber back swayed the fierce wild

red-haired warrior's savage ship.

Loki sings to the raging, passing waves,

and whiffs of blood exhale from Loki's song.

As the hymn of steel soars into space

and its echoes are answered with a fateful din,

and from the pit of the holy deeps the victim seeks,

his stiff arms outstretched, the shadow of the God,

to pale Death passing Loki sings,

and whiffs of blood exhale from Loki's song.

---

[1]Loki is destroyer, friend to Odin and Thor, Promethean thief, shape shifter, magician, and trickster. A giant by parentage, he became a quasi deity and the leader (here, Shepherd) of the frost giants. Loki ultimately would lead the minions of evil against Odin and the forces of good—Aesir—at Ragnarok, the apocalyptic showdown of the Norse cosmos.

Las voces tristes

Por las blancas estepas
se desliza el trineo;
los lejanos aullidos de los lobos
se unen al jadeante resoplar de los perros.

Nieva.
Parece que el espacio se envolviera en un velo,
tachonado de lirios
por las alas del cierzo.

El infinito blanco . . .
sobre el vasto desierto
flota una vaga sensación de angustia,
de supremo abandono, de profundo y sombrío desaliento.

Un pino solitario
dibújase a lo lejos,
en un fondo de brumas y de nieve,
como un largo esqueleto.

Entre los dos sudarios
de la tierra y el cielo,
avanza en el naciente,
el helado crepúsculo de invierno . . .

The Doleful Cries

Over the white steppes
slides the sled;
the far-off howling of the wolves
mingles with the breathless panting of the dogs.

Snow falls.
Space seems shrouded in a veil,
studded with lilies
winging on the cold north wind.

Infinite white . . .
Over the vast wasteland
floats a dim feeling of anguish,
of utter forsakenness, of the deep gloom of losing heart.

A lone pine
appears in the distance
against a background of mists and snow
like a long skeleton.

Between the two shrouds
of earth and sky,
the frozen dawn of winter
makes its way from the east . . .

Lo fugaz

La rosa temblorosa
se desprendió del tallo,
y la arrastró la brisa
sobre las aguas turbias del pantano.

Una onda fugitiva
le abrió su seno amargo,
y estrechando a la rosa temblorosa
la deshizo en sus brazos.

Flotaron sobre el agua
las hojas como miembros mutilados,
y confundidas con el lodo negro,
negras, aun más que el lodo, se tornaron.

Pero en las noches puras y serenas
se sentía vagar en el espacio
un leve olor de rosa
sobre las aguas turbias del pantano.

Ephemera

The quivering rose
broke free from its stem,
and the breeze swept it off
over the murky waters of the marsh.

A wave here and gone
slit the flower's bitter breast;
it took the quivering rose in its embrace,
and tore it limb from limb in its arms.

The dismembered petals floated
mutilated on the waters;
muddled with the black mire,
they turned blacker than the mud itself.

But of an evening clear and calm
drifting through space could be scented
a hint of rose
over the murky waters of the marsh.

Amado Nervo

Amado Nervo (1870–1919) was the most accessible of the modernistas. For this reason—and because of his enormous output—his work has sometimes been called uneven, even superficial, marred by occasional lapses into a somewhat saccharine piety of tone. It is just as true, though, that the Mexican's best poems achieve serenity, a deep spirituality, and impart a consoling humanity: prayerful poems that take the form of quiet meditations, grieving plaints, or ecstatic celebrations. Christian in essence—he had intended to enter the priesthood—Nervo found poetry in oriental thought and frequently approaches Buddhistic doctrine in his treatment of nothingness, compassion, materiality, and desire. A mystic, pantheistic impulse has been noted in such writings as *La hermana agua* ("Sister Water"). But, as José Olivio Jiménez sums up, Nervo's dialectical inner struggle dominated his poetry "entre la carne y el espíritu, la sensualidad y la religiosidad, el impulso exótico y el afán de trascendencia, la fe rota y la necesidad de creer, el desasosiego de los humanos límites . . . y la voluntad de infinitud y paz para el espíritu"(258; "between flesh and spirit, sensuality and spirituality, the erotic impulse and the urge to transcend, broken faith and the need to believe, uneasiness with human limits . . . and the wish for boundlessness and peace for the spirit").

"Edelweiss" features a stylized, erotic creation scene. In "Al cruzar los caminos" ("At the Crossroads"), the narrator lyricizes detachment from "the horror of thought."

Elevación (1917; "Rapture [or Uplifting]") is probably Nervo's most accomplished collection of poetry, though Nervo wrote many short stories, short novels, and journalistic pieces of note, besides an early biography of Sor Juana Inés de la Cruz.

Edelweiss

Sería en los yermos de la blanca Siberia, o del Spitzberg solitario en la inviolada paz. Sobre los témpanos azulados, reverberantes a la luz cobriza de un segmento de sol, levantaría su blanca mole un castillo:

Un castillo de nieve
con almenas de nieve,
rey feudal torvo y frío.

(*En el confín, la aurora boreal difundiría sus nácares.*)

Tú, la castellana, la virgen condesa, adormecida en sueños blancos, ignorada y feliz, inmarcesible flor de las nieves, el prestigioso cáliz abrirías. ¡Qué perfume tan casto en el silencio hiperbóreo desprendieras!

Un perfume süave
—las estrellas son lirios—:
un perfume de estrellas.

(*En el azul, la aurora boreal desataría sus rosas.*)

Labrara mi numen su mejor estrofa: la estrofa virgen, la estrofa eterna, el verbo no encarnado todavía y que flota en el caos de la idea, como Dios sobre el abismo.

Edelweiss

It might be in the wastelands of white Siberia, or of

solitary Spitzberg in its inviolate peacefulness. Over the

bluish ice floes shimmering in the copper light of a shaft of

sun, a castle would rear its hulking white form:

A castle made of snow

with battlements of snow,

a feudal king fierce and cold.

(In the eye's horizon, the aurora borealis would cast its mother-of-pearl.)

You, Spanish woman, virgin countess, slumbering in white

dreams, unsuspected and happy, unfading flower of the snows,

would open the worthy petals. What a chaste perfume you would

give off in the hyperborean silence![1]

A subtle perfume

—the stars are lilies—:

a perfume made of stars.

(In the blue, the aurora borealis would let loose its roses.)

My numen would craft its greatest stanza: the virgin

stanza, the eternal stanza, the word-not-yet-made-flesh,

floating in the chaos of thought, like God over the abyss.

---

[1]Hyperboreans, in classical mythology, were a people who lived in a land of perpetual sunshine and abundance beyond the north wind. A hyperborean may also be an inhabitant of a far northern region.

¡Qué singular morada!

¡Qué ideal moradora!

¡Qué penetrante ritmo!

(*En el cenit, la aurora boreal dardearía sus llamas.*)

What a unique dwelling!

What an ideal occupant!

What a penetrating rhythm!

(*In the zenith, the aurora borealis would dart out its tongues of fire.*)

Al cruzar los caminos

Al cruzar los caminos, el viajero decía
—mientras, lento, su báculo con tedioso compás
las malezas hollaba, los guijarros hería—;
al cruzar los caminos, el viajero decía:
«¡He matado al Anhelo, para siempre jamás!

«¡Nada quiero, ya nada, ni el azul ni la lluvia,
ni las moras de agosto ni las fresas de abril,
ni amar yo a la trigueña ni que me ame la rubia,
ni alabanza de docto ni zalema de vil!

«Nada quiero, ya nada, ni salud ni dinero,
ni alegría, ni gloria, ni esperanza, ni luz.
¡Que me olviden los hombres, y en cualquier agujero
se deshaga mi carne sin estela ni cruz!

«Nada quiero, ya nada, ni el laurel ni la rosa,
ni cosecha en el campo ni bonanza en el mar,
ni sultana ni sierva, ni querida ni esposa,
ni amistad ni respeto . . . Sólo pido una cosa:
¡Que me libres, oh Arcano, del horror de pensar!

«Que me libres, ¡oh Arcano!, del demonio consciente;
que a fundirse contigo se reduzca mi afán,
y el perfume de mi alma suba a ti mudamente.
Sea yo como el árbol y la espiga y la fuente,
que se dan en silencio, sin saber que se dan.»

At the Crossroads

At the crossroads, the traveler said
—as slowly his walking stick, in a tedious rhythm
trod the weeds, the pebbles offending—
at the crossroads, the traveler said:
"I have slain Desire, forever and ever!

"Nothing do I want, nothing, neither the blue nor the rain,
neither the blackberries of August nor the strawberries of April,
neither to love the olive-skinned girl nor for the blonde to love me,
neither praise from the learned nor bows from the lowly!

"Nothing do I want, nothing anymore, neither health nor money,
nor joy, nor glory, nor hope, nor light.
Let men forget me, and my flesh
rot away in any old ditch, without a trace or cross!

"Nothing do I want, nothing anymore, neither crowns of laurel nor
the rose,
neither harvest in the fields nor bounty from the sea,
neither sultana nor servant girl; neither sweetheart nor a wife,
nor friendship, nor respect . . . Only one thing do I ask:
that you free me, O Mystery, from the horror of thought!

"Free me, O Mystery!, from the demon consciousness;
may my ardor cool by its fusing with you,
and the perfume of my soul rise to you without a sound.
May I be like the tree and the stalk of wheat and the spring,
which meet in silence, not knowing that they meet."

José Juan Tablada

José Juan Tablada (1871–1945) was one of the pioneers in bringing the modernista ethos to Mexico, but he is best known today as the poet who introduced the haiku to Spanish. His name is linked to both the orientalist vein of poetry and the avant-garde currents in Spanish America. His innovative ideograms or pictographic poems (e.g., *Li-Po y otros poemas* [1920; "'Li Po' and Other Poems"])—concrete poems shaped like teacups, roses, bamboo groves, and even the staggering path of a poet drunk on wine—still delight readers. Tablada's poems in this style were roughly contemporary with the *calligrammes* of the French writer Guillaume Apollinaire (1880–1918). Two of the Mexican's early volumes, *El florilegio* (1899; "Florilegium") and *Al sol y bajo la luna* (1918; "In the Sun and under the Moon"), are markedly modernista and often treated sexuality with a then-scandalous frankness. One of the strongest poems from these important early and middle periods, a foundational poem for modernismo, is "Onix" ("Onyx"), which depicts a state of abulia and faithlessness. This period also saw the major poem "El poema de Hokusai" ("Hokusai Poem"). Tablada's later poetry embraced Mexican motifs and themes, frequently mixing timeless autochthonous images with historical and political realities, as in his "El ídolo en el atrio" ("The Idol in the Courtyard").

Here we include "Misa negra" (1899; "Black Mass"), a Baudelairean poem that caused a furor at the time. The narrator of the second poem collected here, "Quinta Avenida" (1918; "Fifth Avenue"), a work originally titled ". . . ?," indicts the "hijas de la mecánica Venus made in América" ("daughters of the mechanical, MADE IN USA Venus"). The poem's tone and topos recall the author's "Lawn-Tennis" published the same year, a text that is thematically and lexically modernista but formally avant-garde. Finally, Tablada's idiosyncratic and intuitive haiku from 1919 (*Un día . . . poemas sintéticos* ["One Day . . . Synthetic Poems"]) and 1922 (*El jarro de flores* ["The Flower Vase"]) are represented.

At different points a sympathizer of both Porfirio Díaz and Victoriano Huerta during the Mexican Revolution, the writer had much of his exotic collections and some writings destroyed by Emiliano Zapata's troops. In 1914 Tablada was forced into exile in the United States, where he died in 1945.

Misa negra

¡Noche de sábado! Callada
está la tierra y negro el cielo;
late en mi pecho una balada
de doloroso ritornelo.

El corazón desangra herido
bajo el cilicio de las penas
y corre el plomo derretido
de la neurosis en mis venas.

¡Amada ven! . . . ¡Dale a mi frente
el edredón de tu regazo
y a mi locura dulcemente,
lleva a la cárcel de tu abrazo!

¡Noche de sábado! En tu alcoba
hay perfume de incensario,
el oro brilla y la caoba
tiene penumbras de sagrario.

Y allá en el lecho do reposa
tu cuerpo blanco, reverbera
como custodia esplendorosa
tu desatada cabellera.

Black Mass

Sabbath night! A hush
o'er the earth, and the sky is black;
in my breast beats a ballad
with a grievous ritornello.

My heart bleeds, wounded
by this hairshirt of sorrows,
and the hot lead of neurosis
courses through my veins.

Come, my beloved! Lay my head
down in your eiderdown lap
and sweetly lock my madness up
in the jail of your embrace!

Sabbath night! In your chamber,
perfumes from the censer;
gold is glittering and mahogany
throws the shadows of a shrine.

And there in the bed where
your white body lies,
your flowing tresses
like a dazzling monstrance gleam.

Toma el aspecto triste y frío
de la enlutada religiosa
y con el traje más sombrío
viste tu carne voluptuosa.

Con el murmullo de los rezos
quiero la voz de tu ternura,
y con el óleo de mis besos
ungir de diosa tu hermosura.

Quiero cambiar el grito ardiente
de mis estrofas de otros días,
por la salmodia reverente
de las unciosas letanías;

quiero en las gradas de tu lecho
doblar temblando la rodilla
y hacer del ara de tu lecho
y de tu alcoba la capilla . . .

Y celebrar ferviente y mudo,
sobre tu cuerpo seductor,
lleno de esencias y desnudo
¡la Misa Negra de mi amor!

It takes on the cold, sad air
of a mourning nun,
and in the duskiest dress
your voluptuous flesh is robed.

With whispered prayers
I seek the voice of your tenderness,
and with the holy oil of my kisses
I want to anoint your beauty as a goddess.

I want to trade the passion cry
of my verse from younger days
for the reverent, droning
unction of the litanies;

I want to bend on trembling knee
on the stairsteps to your bed
and to make a chapel
of your altar-bed, your chamber . . .

And burning, silent,
on your seductress body
naked, redolent of essences,
to hold the Black Mass of my love!

Quinta Avenida

Mujeres que pasáis por la Quinta Avenida
tan cerca de mis ojos, tan lejos de mi vida . . .

¿Soñáis desnudas que en el baño os cae
áureo Jove pluvial, ¡como a Danae! . . .
o por ser impregnadas de un tesoro,
al asalto de un toro de oro
tendéis las ancas como Pasifae?

¿Sobáis con perversiones de cornac
de broncíneo elefante la trompa metálica
o transmutáis, urentes, de Karnak
la sala hipóstila, en fálica?

Mujeres fire-proof a la pasión inertes,
hijas de la mecánica Venus made in América;

de vuestra fortaleza, la de las cajas fuertes,
es el secreto ¡idéntica combinación numérica!

Fifth Avenue

You women on Fifth Avenue passing by,
so far from my life, and so close to my eyes . . .

Do you dream, nude, that golden Jupiter rains down
on you in the bath—as he did on Danaë!—
or, for the sake of being impregnated with a treasure,
ravished by a golden bull,
that you spread your haunches like Pasiphaë?[1]

Do you stroke the metallic trunk of bronze elephants
with a tamer's perversions,
or, burning, do you transmute the hypostyle hall at Karnak[2]
into phallic columns?

Fireproof women passive to passion,
daughters of the mechanical, MADE IN USA Venus;

The secret way into your fortress that holds your safes
is the identical combination!

---

[1]Danaë, daughter of King Acrisius of Argos, was imprisoned because the king was told she would bear a son who would kill him. Jupiter came to her as a shower of gold and left her with child (Perseus). When Pasiphaë, wife of King Minos, offended Poseidon, the god inspired her passion for a bull. She mated with the beast in the Labyrinth and gave birth to the Minotaur, which fed on human sacrifices.

[2]Karnak is a massive temple complex on the Nile in Egypt, famed in part for its 134 colossal hieroglyphic columns.

Haikai (selectos)

Pavo real, largo fulgor,
por el gallinero demócrata
pasas como una procesión

—Devuelve a la desnuda rama,
nocturna mariposa,
las hojas secas de tus alas!

El pequeño mono me mira . . .
Quisiera decirme
algo que se le olvida!

Bajo mi ventana, la luna en los tejados,
y las sombras chinescas
y la música china de los gatos.

Busco en vano en la carta
de adiós irremediable
la huella de una lágrima.

Selected Haiku

Peacock, long shining,
through democratic henhouse
like a procession

"Butterfly of night,
give back to naked branches
your wings of dead leaves."

Little monkey looks
at me . . . and longs to tell me
something he forgot!

Under my window the moon on rooftops.
Chinese music of the cats,
the Chinese shadows.

I search the letter,
the final good-bye. In vain:
no signs of a tear.

Enrique González Martínez

Enrique González Martínez (1871–1952), nominated for the Nobel Prize for Literature in 1949, has been variously described as the last modernista and as a transitional figure into the period that followed. He was an important part of the Ateneo de la Juventud, the athenaeum, or cultural organization, that fostered the great literary lights of Mexico at the time, including Alfonso Reyes, José Vasconcelos, and the Dominican writer Pedro Henríquez Ureña. A doctor, politician, translator, and journalist—the precarious economies of Latin America have produced many lifelong polymaths—he was a presence in Mexico until well into the twentieth century.

His famous "Tuércele el cuello al cisne . . ."("Wring the Neck of the Swan . . ."), like José Asunción Silva's "Sinfonía color de fresas con leche" ("Strawberries-and-Milk-Colored Symphony"), has been misunderstood by legions of readers as a dismissal of Rubén Darío. In fact, it was aimed at the Nicaraguan bard's many imitators who abused the more cosmetic of his images and the preciosity of his poetic arsenal. The 1911 poem, which deliberately recalls Paul Verlaine's "Prends l'éloquence et tords-lui son cou!" ("Take eloquence and wring its neck," in "Art poétique" [1882]), rhetorically proposes the wise and penetrating but ungraceful owl—reader of "el misterioso libro del silencio nocturno" ("the mystery book of quiet night")—as a replacement for the ambiguous, androgynous Olympian bird. Indeed, the meditative always predominated over the decorative in his own poetry. "Busca en todas las cosas" ("Seek Out in All Things") represents the moral-didactic vein of modernista aesthetics and some of its attendant conceits, including the exhortation to beauty and the notion of the artist as decipherer of a riddling universe.

Tuércele el cuello al cisne . . .

Tuércele el cuello al cisne de engañoso plumaje
que da su nota blanca al azul de la fuente;
él pasea su gracia no más, pero no siente
el alma de las cosas ni la voz del paisaje.

Huye de toda forma y de todo lenguaje
que no vayan acordes con el ritmo latente
de la vida profunda . . . y adora intensamente
la vida, y que la vida comprenda tu homenaje.

Mira al sapiente búho cómo tiende las alas
desde el Olimpo, deja el regazo de Palas
y posa en aquel árbol el vuelo taciturno . . .

El no tiene la gracia del cisne, mas su inquieta
pupila, que se clava en la sombra, interpreta
el misterioso libro del silencio nocturno.

Wring the Neck of the Swan . . .

Wring the neck of the swan with his feathers false,
the swan who sets a tone of white by fountain's blue;
he but parades his grace, though touching not
the soul of things, nor hearing nature's voice.

Shun the forms and language, all
that are out of tune with secret vital rhythms deep,
. . . and with passion worship life,
and may life acknowledge this, your tribute paid.

Behold the wise old owl, and how he spreads his wings
up on Olympus, flies from Minerva's coddling hand
and on treetop down from gloomy, wordless flight he lights . . .

In swanlike grace the owl's no match,
but his roving eye, which penetrates the dark, makes sense
of the mystery book of quiet night.

Busca en todas las cosas

Busca en todas las cosas un alma y un sentido
oculto; no te ciñas a la apariencia vana;
husmea, sigue el rastro de la verdad arcana,
escudriñante el ojo y aguzado el oído.

No seas como el necio, que al mirar la virgínea
imperfección del mármol que la arcilla aprisiona,
queda sordo a la entraña de la piedra, que entona
en recóndito ritmo la canción de la línea.

Ama todo lo grácil de la vida, la calma
de la flor que se mece, el color, el paisaje.
Ya sabrás poco a poco descifrar su lenguaje . . .
¡Oh divino coloquio de las cosas y el alma!

Hay en todos los seres una blanda sonrisa,
un dolor inefable o un misterio sombrío.
¿Sabes tú si son lágrimas las gotas de rocío?
¿Sabes tú qué secreto va contando la brisa?

Atan hebras sutiles a las cosas distantes;
al acento lejano corresponde otro acento.
¿Sabes tú donde lleva los suspiros el viento?
¿Sabes tú si son almas las estrellas errantes?

Search Out in All Things

Search out in all things a soul
and a hidden meaning; cling not to vain surfaces;
sniff out and follow the trail of arcane truth,
scrutinizing eye and ear attuned.

Be not like the fool, who sees the virginal
flaw in the marble held captive in the clay,
and is deaf to the rock's inner core, which intones
in secret rhythms the song that courses through its vein.

Love all things delicate and graceful in life,
the calm of the swaying flower, color, scenery.
Piece by piece you'll puzzle out their language . . .
O divine colloquy of matter and soul!

In all creation there is a tender smile,
an ineffable pain, or a dark mystery.
Do you know if dewdrops are tears?
Do you know what secret the breeze blows around?

Airy threads are tied to things afar;
one distant sound matches another.
Do you know where the wind takes the sighs it carries off?
Do you know if the wandering stars are souls?

No desdeñes al pájaro de argentina garganta
que se queja en la tarde, que salmodia a la aurora.
Es un alma que canta y es un alma que llora . . .
¡Y sabrá por qué llora, y sabrá por qué canta!

Busca en todas las cosas el oculto sentido;
lo hallarás cuando logres comprender su lenguaje;
cuando sientas el alma colosal del paisaje
y los ayes lanzados por el árbol herido . . .

Scorn not the silver-throated bird

in his evening plaint, or as he drones at dawn.

It is a soul that sings, it is a soul that weeps . . .

And he shall know why he weeps, and he shall know why he sings!

Search out in all things a hidden meaning;

you shall find it when you can unlock their language;

when you feel the colossal soul of nature

and the wounded tree's lament . . .

Guillermo Valencia

A lifelong politician and man of extraordinarily wide-ranging and profound erudition, the Colombian Guillermo Valencia (1873–1943) was responsible for many enduring modernista poems, among them "A Popayán" ("To Popayan"), "Las dos cabezas" ("The Two Heads"), "Los camellos" ("The Camels"), and "San Antonio y el centauro" ("Saint Anthony and the Centaur"), the last of which mingles pagan and Christian elements. His *Ritos* ("Rites") from 1899 remains a watershed work in the formation of modernista aesthetics. He was an important translator of Parnassian and symbolist authors. Valencia's 1929 book *Catay* ("Cathay") consisted of versions of Li Po, Tu Fu, and others from the Chinese, a language he depended on trots—an informant's glosses—in order to render into Spanish. Although guided by a strict moral compass, in all his work he was a consummate stylist with a musical ear and a Parnassian sense of form. In his famous paean to José Asunción Silva, "Leyendo a Silva" ("Reading Silva"), he attributed to his tragic compatriot the supreme valuation of form—often applied to Valencia himself—in the phrase "sacrificar un mundo para pulir un verso" ("to sacrifice a world to polish a verse").

Many of the poet's themes—the artist's alienation, the insensitivity of the masses, inner conflict over competing ideas—appear in "Cigüeñas blancas" ("White Storks"), excerpted here. In "Anarkos" ("Anarchos"), whose title is from the Greek for "leaderless" or "lawlessness," we find a committed poem sympathetic to the disenfranchised. Valencia, a master orator, used the stirring populist poem in his presidential campaigning. Significantly, it contains an emblem dear to the modernistas—the precious gem—but with an ironic inversion: here it is the suffering worker in the mines who cannot attain what he risks his life to extract. We include "Anarchos" to reveal a self-critical side to modernismo.

Cigüeñas blancas (fragmentos)

Ciconia pietatis cultrix . . .
—Petronio

De cigüeñas la tímida bandada
recogiendo las alas blandamente
paró sobre la torre abandonada
a la luz del crepúsculo muriente;

hora en que el Mago de feliz paleta
vierte bajo la cúpula radiante
pálidos tintes de fugaz violeta
que riza con su soplo el aura errante.

Esas aves me inquietan: en el alma
reconstruyen mis rotas alegrías;
evocan en mi espíritu la calma,
la augusta calma de mejores días.

Afrenta la negrura de sus ojos
al abenuz de tonos encendidos,
y van los picos de matices rojos
a sus gargantas de alabastro unidos.

White Storks (excerpts)

Ciconia pietatis cultrix . . .
—*Petronius*

The shy flock of storks
gently gather in their wings
and perch on the abandoned turret
in the failing light of dusk;

the hour when the Magus, his palette rejoiced,
under the luminous cupola
sheds pale and fleeting violet hues
which the wayward zephyr ripples with its breath of wind.

These birds unease me: in my soul
they build my broken joys back up;
they call calm into my spirit,
the august calm of better days.

The blackness of their eyes
offends the burning tones of ebony,
and red-hued beaks move in unison
with their alabaster throats.

The Latin epigraph means "the stork, cultivator of piety." It comes from book 8 of Petronius's *Satyricon*: "Ciconia etiam, grata peregrina hospita / pietaticultrix, gracilipes, crotalistria" ("Even the kindly stork is sacrificed, / Our graceful, noisy, long-legged friend" [trans. Alfred R. Allinson]). Petronius (27–66 CE) was a Roman satirist who famously slashed his wrists in a slow suicide.

Vago signo de mística tristeza
es el perfil de su sedoso flanco
que evoca, cuando al sol se despereza,
las lentas agonías de lo Blanco.

Con la veste de mágica blancura,
con el talle de lánguido diseño,
semeja en el espacio su figura
el pálido estandarte del Ensueño.

Y si, huyendo la garra que la acecha,
el ala encoge, la cabeza extiende,
parece un arco de rojiza flecha
que oculta mano en el espacio tiende.

A los fulgores de sidérea lumbre,
en el vaivén de su cansado vuelo,
fingen, bajo la cóncava techumbre
bacantes del azul ebrias de cielo . . .

. . . .

Todo tiene sus aves: la floresta,
de mirlos guarda deliciosos dúos;
el torreón de carcomida testa
oye la carcajada de los búhos;

Vague sign of mystic sadness
is the outline of their silken flanks
that when stretched out in the sun evoke
the slow death throes of all things white.

With their vestments of magic whiteness,
with the languid build of their design,
their figures look in space
like Reverie's pallid banners.

And when fleeing clutches giving chase,
they tuck their wings, stick out their heads,
and look like bows with copper-colored arrows drawn
back by an unseen hand in space.

By the starshine's light,
in the to and fro of their weary flight,
under the concave vault they make like
sky-drunk bacchants of the blue . . .

. . . .

Everything has its birds: the jungle
houses lovely duets of blackbirds;
from its tumble-down heights the tower
harks to the hearty laughing owls:

la Gloria tiene al águila bravía:
albo coro de cisnes los Amores;
tienen los montes que la nieve enfría
la estirpe colosal de los condores;

y de lo Viejo en el borroso escudo
—reliquia de volcado poderío—
su cuello erige en el espacio mudo
ella, ¡la novia lánguida del Frío!

La cigüeña es el alma del Pasado,
es la Piedad, es el Amor ya ido;
mas su velo también está manchado
y el numen del candor, envejecido.

¡Perlas, cubrid el ceñidor oscuro
que ennegrece la pompa de sus galas!
¡Detén, Olvido, el oleaje impuro
que ha manchado la albura de sus alas!

. . . .

Si pudiesen, asidos de tu manto,
ir, en las torres a labrar el nido;
si curase la llaga de su canto
el pensamiento de futuro olvido;

Glory has the wild eagle:
Love, its white choir of swans;
the mountains chilled from the frozen snows
have the colossal stock of the condor;

and from ancient times on the misty shield
—a relic of hollowed might—
she, the languid bride of Winter!,
stretches up her neck in silent space.

The stork is the soul of the Past,
she is Mercy, and Love grown cold;
but her veil is sullied too,
and the numen of her whiteness, aged.

Pearls, conceal the dim girdle
that darkens the splendor of her bridal gown!
Stay, O Lethean waters, the impure surge
that has blighted her white wings!

. . . .

If they could, taking hold the cloak,
go into the towers to build their nest;
if the wound of their song were cured
by the thought of future forgetting;

¡ah!, si supiesen que el soñado verso,
el verso de oro que les dé la palma
y conquiste, vibrando, el universo,
¡oculto muere sin salir del alma!

Cantar, soñar . . . conmovedor delirio,
deleite para el vulgo; amargas penas
a que nadie responde; atroz martirio
de Petronio cortándose las venas . . .

¡Oh poetas! Enfermos escultores
que hacen la forma con esmero pulcro,
¡y consumen los prístinos albores
cincelando su lóbrego sepulcro!

Aves que arrebatáis mi pensamiento
al limbo de las formas; divo soplo
traiga desde vosotras manso viento
a consagrar los filos de mi escoplo:

amo los vates de felina zarpa
que acendran en sus filos amargura
y lívido corcel, mueven el arpa
a la histérica voz de su locura.

Dadme el verso pulido en alabastro,
que rígido y exangüe, como el ciego

oh! if they knew that the dreamed-of verse,
the verse of gold that earns them the prize
and conquers the universe, vibrant,
dies unknown, issueless inside the soul!

To sing, to dream . . . , stirring frenzy,
delight for the masses; bitter sorrows
that receive no response; a cruel martyrdom
of Petronius slitting his veins . . .

O poets! Sick sculptors
who are creators of forms of exquisite art,
and work away the pristine dawns
carving their gloomy tombs!

Birds that carry off my thoughts from me
to the Limbo of forms; may a breath of wind
bring from you a gentle breeze
to consecrate my chisel's edge:

I love the bards of feline claw
who on statuary curves and chargers pale
refine their grief, and move the harp
to the hysterical voice of their madness.

Give me the polished alabaster verse,
unyielding, bloodless, like the blind

mire sin ojos para ver: un astro
de blanda luz cual cinerario fuego.

¡Busco las rimas en dorada lluvia;
chispa, fuentes, cascada, lagos, ola!
¡Quiero el soneto cual león de Nubia:
de ancha cabeza y resonante cola!

who look sightlessly to see: a star

shining faintly like a funeral pyre.

I seek rhymes in a golden rain;

spark, fountains, waterfall, lakes, and wave!

I want a sonnet like a Nubian lion:

broad-headed and with tail resounding!

Anarkos (fragmento)

Los mudos socavones de las minas
se tragan en falanges los obreros
que, suspendidos sobre abismo loco,
semejan golondrinas
posadas en fantásticos aleros.
Con luz fosforescente de cocuyos,
trémula y amarilla,
perfora oscuridad su lamparilla;
sobre vertiginosos voladeros
acometen olímpicos trabajos,
y en tintas de carbón ennegrecidos,
se clavan en los fríos agujeros,
como un pueblo infeliz de escarabajos
a taladrar los árboles podridos.
Sus manos desgarradas
vierten sangre; sarcástica retumba
la voz en la recóndita huronera:
allí fue su vivir; allí su tumba
les abrirá la bárbara cantera
que inmóvil, dura, sus alientos gasta,
o frenética y ciega y bruta y sorda
con sus olas de piedra los aplasta.

El minero jadeante
mira saltar la chispa de diamante

Anarchos (excerpt)

The voiceless mine shafts

devour the workers phalanx by phalanx.

Suspended over mad abysses,

they look like swallows

perched on dreamlike eaves.

With the trembling yellow

phosphorescent light of fireflies

their little lanterns pierce the gloom;

on dizzying needle-beam scaffolds

they undertake Olympian tasks;

coal-blackened,

they thrust into the cold holes

like a wretched race of beetles

boring into rotten trees.

Their shattered hands

are gushing blood; the sarcastic shouts

thunder deep inside their hiding place:

down into it went their lives; down there a savage quarry

will dig their tomb for them,

a hard unmoving place that gnaws away their spirit,

or frenzied, brutish, blind, and deaf,

will crush them under wave after wave of rock.

The breathless miner

watches as the tiny diamond comes loose,

que años después envidiará su hija,
cuando triste y hambrienta y haraposa,
la mejilla más blanca que una rosa
blanca, y el ojo con azul ojera,
se pare a remirarla, codiciosa,
al través de una diáfana vidriera,
do mágicos joyeles
en rubias sedas y olorosas pieles
fulgen: piedras de trémulos cambiantes,
ligadas por artistas
en cintillos: rubíes y amatistas,
zafiros y brillantes,
la perla oscura y el topacio gualda,
y en su mórbido estuche
de rojizo peluche,
como vivo retoño, la esmeralda.
La joven, pensativa,
sus ojos clava, de un azul intenso,
en las joyas, cautiva
de algo que duerme entre el tesoro inmenso;
no es la codicia sórdida que labra
el pecho de los viles:
es que la dicen mística palabra
las gemas que tallaron los buriles:
ellas proclaman la fatiga ignota
de los mineros, acosada estirpe
que sobre recio pedernal se agota,

years hence the object of his daughter's envy,
when sad and hungry, dressed in tatters,
her cheek whiter than a white rose,
and dark-blue circles under her eyes,
covetous, she'll stop to gaze long and hard
through the transparent showcase glass.
Magical little jewels lie sparkling there
on golden silks and fur sweet-smelling:
iridescing stones, and flickering,
set by artists
into rings: rubies and amethysts,
sapphires and diamonds,
dark pearl and yellow topaz,
and sitting in its delicate case
of reddish plush,
like a living bud, the emerald.
The girl, lost in thought,
fixes her gaze, her eyes burning blue,
on the gems, in thrall
to something slumbering within the vast treasure;
it is not the vile covetousness that chisels
the heart of the villainous:
but that the burin-carved gems
speak to her a mystical message:
they proclaim the miners'
unknown fatigue; a persecuted tribe are they,
ground down on the hard flint,

destrozada la faz, el alma rota,
sin un caudillo que su mal extirpe:

El diamante es el lloro
de la raza minera
en los antros más hondos de la hullera:

¡loor a los valientes campeones
que vertieron sus lágrimas
entre los socavones!

Es el rubí la sangre
de los héroes que, en épicas faenas,
tiñeron el filón con el desangre
que hurtó la vida a sus hinchadas venas:

¡loor a los valientes campeones
que perdieron sus vidas
entre los socavones!

El zafiro recuerda
a los trabajadores de las simas
el último jirón de cielo puro
que vieron al mecerse de la cuerda
que los bajaba al laberinto oscuro:

their faces wracked, their soul in ruins,
without a leader to cure their ills:

Diamonds are the tears
of the miners' race
in the deepest of the coal mine's caverns:

praised be the valiant heroes
who shed their tears
down in the shafts!

The ruby is the blood
of the heroes whose blood loss
stained the seam on epic jobs,
and sapped the life from their distended veins:

praised be the brave champions
who lost their lives
down in the shafts!

The sapphire reminds
the workers in the depths
of the last patch of clear sky
they glimpsed from the swaying rope
that lowered them down into the dark labyrinth:

¡loor a los sepultos campeones
que no verán ya el cielo
entre los socavones!

Y el topacio de tinte amarillento
es recóndita ira
y concreciones de dolor; lamento
que entre el callado boquerón expira:

¡loor a los cautivos campeones
que como fieras rugen
entre los socavones!

La joven pordiosera
huyó . . .

praised be the buried heroes
who shall not see the sky
from inside the shafts!

And the yellow-tinged topaz
is secret wrath,
concretions of woe; a wail, a dying breath
exhaled through the silent opening above:

praised be the captive heroes
who roar like wild beasts
down in the shafts!

The beggar girl
has fled . . .

José María Eguren

Strange, abstract, and compelling, the work of the reclusive Peruvian poet José María Eguren (1874–1942) evinces Nordic children's literature, the French and Italian decadents and symbolists, and the English painters of the aestheticist school. Also a watercolorist of note, Eguren infused impressionistic, dreamlike qualities into lyrics like those of the medieval ballads. His is a hermetic body of work that conjures subtly other-world protagonists: a dead puppet in his funeral procession; a tired god wandering through the lands of progress and atheism; the dark night walker foretelling war; the "bárbara y dulce princesa de Viena" ("sweet, barbaric princess of Vienna") with her blue flowers of insanity.

Here we present three poems from *Simbólica* (1911; "Symbolics"): "Marcha fúnebre de una Marionnette" ("Funeral March of a Marionette"), a wistful elegy; the cryptic "Los reyes rojos" ("The Red Kings"); and "La dama i" ("Lady i"), which in technique recalls the Pre-Raphaelites. "Peregrín cazador de figuras" (1916; "Peregrine the Image Hunter") projects the poet as a privileged seer of nocturnal—unconscious? inner?—visions.

Eguren's painterly symbolism was not fully appreciated until after the modernista period, in part since his native Peru at the time thought his countryman José Santos Chocano's bombast was the paragon of good poetry; if Santos Chocano was modernismo's trumpeter, Eguren was its harpist.

Marcha fúnebre de una Marionnette

Suena trompa del infante con aguda melodía . . .
La farándula ha llegado de la reina Fantasía;
y en las luces otoñales se levanta plañidera
la carroza delantera.
Pasan luego, a la sordina, peregrinos y lacayos
y con sus caparazones los acéfalos caballos;
va en azul melancolía
la muñeca. ¡No hagáis ruido!;
se diría, se diría
que la pobre se ha dormido.
Vienen túmidos y erguidos palaciegos borgoñones
y los siguen arlequines con estrechos pantalones.
Ya monótona en litera
va la reina de madera;
y Paquita siente anhelo de reír y de bailar,
flotó breve la cadencia de la murria y la añoranza;
suena el pífano campestre con los aires de la danza.
¡Pobre, pobre marionnette que la van a sepultar!
Con silente poesía
va un grotesco Rey de Hungría
y lo siguen los alanos;

Funeral March of a Marionette

The prince's horn sounds with a melody shrill . . .

Queen Phantasy has sent her strolling players;

and in the autumn colors the plaintive funeral coach

is raised and takes up the lead.

Then pilgrims and laymen pass by on the quiet,

acephalic harnessed horses in their finery pass by too,

with azure melancholy

does the little puppet pass. Hush, now, everyone!

One would think, one would think

the poor thing is asleep.

Puffed up with pride come the swollen Burgundian courtiers

and in tow come harlequins in skin-tight pants.

Monotonous, on her litter borne,

the wooden queen goes past;

and Francie longs to laugh and dance,

fleet floated the cadence of soul-sick loss and lonely grief;

the country fife plays the tunes for dance.

Poor, poor marionette, she's going to be buried!

With unspoken poetry

a grotesque King of Hungary passes;

the wolfhounds trail behind;

The poem's title is from a ghoulish orchestral work written by the French composer Charles Gounod (1818–93) in 1873. Eguren makes use of other music motifs and references, including the fast Basque dance in 5/8 time, the zortzico.

así toda la jauría

con los viejos cortesanos.

Y en tristor a la distancia

vuelan goces de la infancia,

los amores incipientes, los que nunca han de durar.

¡Pobrecita la muñeca que la van a sepultar!

Melancólico un zorcico se prolonga en la mañana,

la penumbra se difunde por el monte y la llanura,

marionnette deliciosa va a llegar a la temprana

sepultura.

En la trocha aúlla el lobo

cuando gime el melodioso paro bobo.

Tembló el cuerno de la infancia con aguda melodía

y la dicha tempranera a la tumba llega ahora

con funesta poesía

y Paquita danza y llora.

so too the whole pack

of old courtesans.

And, sorrowing, off into the distance

childhood pleasures fly,

first loves, which shall never survive.

Poor little puppet, she's going to be buried!

The melancholic zortzico lasts the morning long,

shadow spreads over mountain and plain,

the delightful marionette is going to an early

grave.

On the trail the wolf howls

as the melodious titmouse moans.

Childhood's horn shook with melody shrill

and youth's happiness leads now to the tomb

with fateful poetry

and Francie dances and sings.

Los reyes rojos

Desde la aurora
combaten dos reyes rojos,
con lanza de oro.

Por verde bosque
y en los purpurinos cerros
vibra su ceño.

Falcones reyes
batallan en lejanías
de oro azulinas.

Por la luz cadmio,
airadas se ven pequeñas
sus formas negras.

Viene la noche
y firmes combaten foscos
los reyes rojos.

The Red Kings

Since dawn
two red kings do battle
with their golden lances.

Through verdant woods,
in purpled hills,
their scowls ring.

Kingly falcons
make war
off in the golden blue beyond.

In the cadmium light
seething, their black forms
seem small.

Come the night,
and the hard unyielding red kings
are battling still.

La dama i

La dama i, vagarosa
en la niebla del lago,
canta las finas trovas.

Va en su góndola encantada
de papel a la misa
verde de la mañana.

Y en su ruta va cogiendo
las dormidas umbelas
y los papiros muertos.

Los sueños rubios de aroma
despierta blandamente
su sardana en las hojas.

Y parte dulce, adormida,
a la borrosa iglesia
de la luz amarilla.

Lady i

Lady i, leisurely
in the misty lake,
sings exquisite ballads of the troubadours.

She is on her way
to the green Mass of morning
in her enchanted paper gondola.

And all along the way she picks
the slumbering umbel flower clusters
and dead papyrus plants.

Their Sardane circle dance in the leaves
gently wakens
aromatic golden dreams.

And sweetly, sleepily, off she goes
to the hazy church
of yellow light.

Peregrín cazador de figuras

En el mirador de la fantasía,

al brillar del perfume

tembloroso de armonía;

en la noche que llamas consume;

cuando duerme el ánade implume,

los órficos insectos se abruman

y luciérnagas fuman;

cuando lucen los silfos galones, entorcho

y vuelan mariposas de corcho

o los rubios vampiros cecean,

o las firmes jorobas campean;

por la noche de los matices,

de ojos muertos y largas narices;

en el mirador distante,

por las llanuras;

Peregrín cazador de figuras

con ojos de diamante

mira desde las ciegas alturas.

Peregrine the Image Hunter

In imagination's lookout
in the twinkling of perfume
quivering harmonic;
in the flame-devoured night,
when the unfledged duck is sleeping,
the Orphic insects throng,
and the fireflies flare and dim;
when the decorated sylphs shine in golden braid
and butterflies of corkwood bark take flight,
when the fair-haired vampires talk in lisps
and the steadfast hunchback girls reconnoiter
in the night of subtle shades,
of eyes that are dead and noses long;
in yonder lookout
on the plains;
Peregrine the image hunter
watches with his diamond eyes
from the unseen heights.

Leopoldo Lugones

A major yet perhaps underrepresented figure in the history of Spanish American letters, Leopoldo Lugones (1874–1938) produced some of the milestones of modernismo: *Las montañas de oro* (1897; "The Mountains of Gold"), *Los crepúsculos del jardín* (1905; "The Twilights of the Garden"), and *Lunario sentimental* (1909; "Lunar Chart of the Heart; or, Sentimental Almanac"). The last, a whole book devoted to reinventions of the moon, marked a transition into the bold new metaphoric leaps of the avant-garde.

An example is from "Jaculatoria lunar" ("Dithyramb to the Moon"): "Luna de oro falso, / . . . / tarántula del diablo, / musa del alcohol, / maléfico vocablo, / perla espectral del sol, / . . . / Danos tu dulce mal" (136–37; "Moon of fool's gold, / . . . / tarantula of the devil, / muse of alcohol, / curse word, / spectral pearl of the sun, / . . . / give us your sweet evil"). Indeed, the metaphor had always been at the core of his poetics. His *Las fuerzas extrañas* (1906; "Strange Forces"), a prose tour de force of the esoterica then in vogue in cosmopolitan Buenos Aires, was a formative text for turn-of-the-century *ciencia ficción* (not Anglo-America's science fiction as such but speculative fantastic tales exploring abnormal psychology, occultist doctrine, and supernatural fantasy). Like many Argentine writers at the time, he also explored the national psyche and social history—for example, in *La guerra gaucha* (1905; "The Gaucho War").

Here we include "A Histeria" ("To Hysteria"), whose innovative form approaches prose poetry; "*Delectación morosa*" ("Sullen Delights"), the title referring to the act—*delectatio morosa*—of taking pleasure in contemplating a sin; a modern ode, "Divagación lunar" ("Lunar Digressions"); "La blanca soledad" ("White Solitude"), an astral valentine to an absent love; and the sepulchral "Historia de mi muerte" ("Story of My Death").

Though an inescapable precursor for whole generations of Argentine writers, including Jorge Luis Borges, who cowrote a book on him in 1965 (Borges and Edelberg) and who complained of his compatriot's baroque penchant for using "todas las palabras del diccionario" (461; "all the words in the dictionary"), Leopoldo Lugones fell out of favor toward the end of his life, having taken a strange turn into fascist sympathy for Argentina's ruling army. Lugones killed himself in 1938, leaving a vast legacy whose importance cannot be overstated. Borges again: "para ser discípulo de Lugones, no es necesario haberlo leído" (461; "to be a disciple of Lugones, one need not have read him").

A Histeria

¡Oh, cómo te miraban las tinieblas, —cuando ciñendo el nudo de tu abrazo—a mi garganta, mientras yo espoleaba—el formidable ijar de aquel caballo, —cruzábamos la selva temblorosa—llevando nuestro horror bajo los astros! —Era una selva larga, toda negra: —la selva dolorosa cuyos gajos—echaban sangre al golpe de las hachas, —como los miembros de un molusco estraño. —Era una selva larga, toda triste, —i en sus sombras reinaba nuestro espanto. —El espumante potro galopaba—mojando de sudores su cansancio, —i ya hacía mil años que corría—por aquel bosque lúgubre. Mil años! —I aquel bosque era largo, largo i triste, —i en sus sombras reinaba nuestro espanto. —I era tu abrazo como nudo de horca, —i eran glaciales témpanos tus labios, —i eran agrios alambres mis tendones, —y eran zarpas retráctiles mis manos, —i era el enorme potro un viento negro—furioso en su carrera de mil años.

Caímos a un abismo tan profundo—que allí no había Dios: montes lejanos—levantaban sus cúspides, casqueadas—
de nieve, bajo el brillo de los astros, —como enormes cabezas
de califas; —describía Saturno un lento arco—sobre el tremendo asombro de la noche; —los solemnes reposos del Océano—desnivelaba la siniestra luna, —i las ondas, hirviendo en los peñascos, hablaban como lenguas, con el grito—de las vidas humanas que tragaron. —Entonces, desatando de mi cuello—el formidable nudo de tu abrazo, —buscaste ansiosa con tus ojos mártires, —mis torvos ojos que anegó el espanto. —Oh, no mires mis ojos; hai un vértigo—

To Hysteria

Oh, how the darkness looked upon you, / as you engirdled your arm / around my throat, while I spurred / that horse's formidable flank, / crossing the trembling woods / dragging our horror under the stars! / It was a long forest, entirely black: / a pained forest, its branches / spouting blood at the blow of the axes, / like the limbs of some strange mollusk. / It was a long forest, entirely sad, / and in its shadows our fright did reign. / The foaming colt galloped, / its fatigue drenched in sweat. / Already for a thousand years had it been running / through those lugubrious woods. A thousand years! / And those woods were long, long and sad, / and in its shadows our fright did reign. / And your embrace was like the ropes of the gallows, / and your lips were glacial tympana, / and my tendons were sour wires, / and my hands were retractile claws, and the enormous colt was a black wind, / enraged in its thousand-year race.

The depths of the abyss / into which we fell measured in the absence of God: distant mountains / raised their peaks, cascades / of snow, beneath the shining stars, / like enormous heads of caliphs; / Saturn traced a slow arch / over the tremendous wonder of the night, / the solemn repose of the Ocean / tilted the sinister moon, / and the waves, boiling in the crags, / spoke like tongues, screaming / of the human lives they had swallowed. / Then, as you untied from my neck / the formidable knot of your embrace, / your martyr eyes searched, anxious, / my grim eyes, filled with fright. / Oh, do not look into my eyes, there is vertigo /

dormido en sus tinieblas; hai relámpagos—de fiebre en sus honduras misteriosas, —i la noche de mi alma más abajo: —una noche cruzada de cometas—que son gigantes pensamientos blancos! —¡Oh, no mires mis ojos, que mis ojos—están sangrientos como dos cadalsos; —negros como dos héroes que velan—enlutados al pié de un catafalco! —I aparecieron dos ojeras tristes—como flores del Mal bajo tus párpados, —i yo besaba las siniestras flores, —i se apretaban tus heladas manos—sobre mi corazón, brasa lasciva, —i alzábanse tus ojos en espasmo, —i yo apartaba mis terribles ojos, —i en tus ojos de luz había llanto, —i mis ojos cerrábanse, implacables, —i tus ojos abríanse, sonámbulos, —i quería mis ojos tu locura, —i huía de tus ojos mi pecado: —i al fin mis fieros ojos, como un crimen, —sobre tus ojos tímidos brillaron, —i al sumergir en mis malditos ojos—el rayo triste de tus ojos pálidos, —en mis brazos quedaste, amortajada, —bajo una eterna frialdad de mármol.

asleep in their darkness; there are lightning bolts / of fever in their mysterious depths, / and the night of my soul further below: / a night crossed with comets: / giant blank thoughts! / Oh, do not look into my eyes, for my eyes / are bloody as two scaffolds; / as two mourning heroes in black / keeping vigil at the foot of a catafalque! / And under the lids your eyes, / like flowers of Evil, two sad circles did appear, / I kissed the sinister flowers, / and your frozen hands tightened / over my heart, that live coal of lust, / and your eyes turned up in a spasm, / and I removed my terrible eyes, / and in your eyes of light there was a cry, / and my eyes closed, implacable, / and your eyes opened, like a sleepwalker's, / and your madness wanted my eyes, / and from your eyes my sin fled: / and at last my savage eyes shined like a crime / over your timid eyes, / and when you plunged into my wicked eyes / the sad ray of your pallid eyes / you fell into my arms, shrouded / under an eternal coldness of marble.

(trans. SW)

Delectación morosa

La tarde, con ligera pincelada
que iluminó la paz de nuestro asilo,
apuntó en su matiz crisoberilo
una sutil decoración morada.

Surgió enorme la luna en la enramada;
las hojas agravaban su sigilo,
y una araña en la punta de su hilo,
tejía sobre el astro, hipnotizada.

Poblóse de murciélagos el combo
cielo, a manera de chinesco biombo;
sus rodillas exangües sobre el plinto

manifestaban la delicia inerte,
y a nuestros pies un río de jacinto
corría sin rumor hacia la muerte.

Sullen Delights

The afternoon, which with a light brushstroke
illuminated the peace of our sanctuary,
drew with a chrysoberyl hue
a subtle decoration of purple.

The moon arose enormous in the arbor;
the leaves aggravated its discretion,
and a spider weaving on the tip of its thread
was hypnotized by the lunarly body.

The curved sky was filled with
bats, like a Chinese folding screen;
your pale, weak knees on the plinth

revealed the inert delight,
and at our feet a river of hyacinth
ran soundless toward death.

(trans. SW)

Divagación lunar

Si tengo la fortuna
de que con tu alma mi dolor se integre,
te diré entre melancólico y alegre
las singulares cosas de la luna.

Mientras el menguante exiguo
a cuyo noble encanto ayer amaste
aumenta su desgaste
de cequín antiguo,
quiero mezclar a tu champaña,
como un buen astrónomo teórico,
su luz, en sensación extraña
de jarabe hidroclórico.
Y cuando te envenene
la pálida mixtura,
como a cualquier romántica Eloísa o lrene,
tu espíritu de amable criatura
buscará una secreta higiene
en la pureza de mi desventura.

Amarilla y flacucha,
la luna cruza el azul pleno,
como una trucha
por un estanque sereno.
Y su luz ligera,
indefiniendo asaz tristes arcanos,

Lunar Digressions

If I may have the fortune

of having your soul reintegrate my pain,

then I shall tell you, from between melancholy and happiness,

of the singular turns of the moon.

While the scant waning

whose noble enchantments, yesterday's love,

increases the wearing away

of its ancient sequin,

I would like to add, like a good theoretical astronomer,

its light to your champagne

to get the strange sensation

of a hydrochloric syrup.

And when I poison

your pale mixture,

like any romantic Eloise or Irene,

your spirit, that of a kind creature,

will search for some secret hygiene

in the purity of my misfortune.

Yellow and skinnish,

the moon crosses the full blue,

as a trout

through a calm pool,

and its swift light,

abundantly undefining sad secrets,

pone una mortuoria traslucidez de cera
en la gemela nieve de tus manos.

Cuando aún no estaba la luna, y afuera
como un corazón poético y sombrío
palpitaba el cielo de primavera,
la noche, sin ti, no era
más que un oscuro frío.
Perdida toda forma, entre tanta
obscuridad, era sólo un aroma;
y el arrullo amoroso ponía en tu garganta
una ronca dulzura de paloma.
En una puerilidad de tactos quedos,
la mirada perdida en una estrella,
me extravié en el roce de tus dedos.
Tu virtud fulminaba como una centella . . .
mas el conjuro de los ruegos vanos
te llevó al lance dulcemente inicuo,
y el coraje se te fue por las manos
como un poco de agua por un mármol oblicuo.

La luna fraternal, con su secreta
intimidad de encanto femenino,
al definirte hermosa te ha vuelto coqueta,
sutiliza tus maneras un complicado tino;
en la lunar presencia,
no hay ya ósculo que el labio al labio suelde;

places a funereal translucence of wax
in the twin snows of your hands.

When the moon had not yet risen, and outside
the spring sky was beating
like a somber and poetic heart,
the night, without you, was nothing
but a dark coldness.
All form having been lost, you were
but an aroma in the entire darkness;
and the loving cooing made of your throat
the sweetness of a dove's crying.
In the puerility of your soft sense of touch,
my gaze lost upon a star,
I was misguided with the brush of your fingers.
Your virtue fulminating like a ray of light . . .
But the incantation of the vain pleas
led to your sweetly unfair flight,
and your courage slipped through your hands
like a bit of water over a slanted slab of marble.

The fraternal moon, with its secret
intimacy of feminine enchantments,
drew your beauty but made you tempting.
A complicated judgment subtilizes your ways;
beneath the lunar presence,
there is no longer a kiss that can weld lip to lip;

y sólo tu seno de audaz incipiencia,
con generosidad rebelde,
continúa el ritmo de la dulce violencia.

Entre un recuerdo de Suiza
y la anécdota de un oportuno primo,
tu crueldad virginal se sutiliza;
y con sumisión postiza
te acurrucas en pérfido mimo,
como un gato que se hace una bola
en la cabal redondez de su cola.

Es tu ilusión suprema
de joven soñadora,
ser la joven mora
de un antiguo poema.
La joven cautiva que llora
llena de luna, de amor y de sistema.

La luna enemiga
que te sugiere tanta mala cosa,
y de mi brazo cordial te desliga,
pone un detalle trágico en tu intriga
de pequeño mamífero rosa.
Mas, al amoroso reclamo
de la tentación, en tu jardín alerta,
tu grácil juventud despierta
golosa de caricia y de «Yoteamo».

and only your daringly incipient bosom,
continues, with rebellious generosity,
the rhythm of the sweet violence.

Between a memory from Switzerland
and the anecdote of an opportune cousin
your virginal cruelty turns even more subtle;
and with false submission
you soften in treacherous indulgence,
like a cat curling up
in the full circling of its tail.

It is your supreme illusion
as a young dreamer,
to be the young Moorish woman
of an ancient poem.
The young captive woman crying
full of moon, of love, and of system.

The enemy moon
which suggests so much evil to you,
and slides you from my cordial arm,
draws a tragic detail in your small
pink mammalian intrigue.
But, at the loving call
of temptation, in your alert garden,
your graceful youth awakens
greed for caress and *Iloveyou*.

En el albaricoque
un tanto marchito de tu mejilla,
pone el amor un leve toque
de carmín, como una lucecilla.
Lucecilla que a medias con la luna
tu rostro excava en escultura inerte,
y con sugestión oportuna
de pronto nos advierte
no sé qué próximo estrago,
como el rizo anacrónico de un lago
anuncia a veces el soplo de la muerte.

In the somewhat faded
apricot of your cheek,
love draws, like a small light,
a touch of carmine crimson.
A small light, complemented by the moon,
which your face shapes into an inert sculpture,
too suddenly alerts us,
with an opportune suggestion,
of unknown upcoming devastation:
much as the anachronic ripplings on a lake
can sometimes announce the breath of death.

(trans. SW)

La blanca soledad

Bajo la calma del sueño,
calma lunar de luminosa seda,
la noche
como si fuera
el blando cuerpo del silencio,
dulcemente en la inmensidad se acuesta . . .
Y desata
su cabellera,
en prodigioso follaje
de alamedas.

Nada vive sino el ojo
del reloj en la torre tétrica,
profundizando inútilmente el infinito
como un agujero abierto en la arena.
El infinito,
rodado por las ruedas
de los relojes,
como un carro que nunca llega.

La luna cava un blanco abismo
de quietud, en cuya cuenca
las cosas son cadáveres
y las sombras viven como ideas.
Y uno se pasma de lo próxima
que está la muerte en la blancura aquella.

White Solitude

In the calm of sleep,
the lunar calm of luminous silk,
night
as if it were
the tender body of silence
gently lays herself down in the vast spaces,
letting down
her hair
in all its marvelous
poplar leafage.

Nothing moves but the eye
of the clock in the gloomy tower,
sounding the infinite in vain
like a hole dug in the sand.
The infinite,
sent spinning by the wheels
of the clocks,
like a carriage that never arrives.

The moon burrows a white abyss
of stillness; in its socket
objects are corpses
and shadows live like ideas.
One marvels at how near
death draws in the whiteness,

De lo bello que es el mundo
poseído por la antigüedad de la luna llena.
Y el ansia tristísima de ser amado,
en el corazón doloroso tiembla.

Hay una ciudad en el aire,
una ciudad casi invisible suspensa,
cuyos vagos perfiles
sobre la clara noche transparentan,
como las rayas de agua en un pliego,
su cristalización poliédrica.
Una ciudad tan lejana,
que angustia con su absurda presencia.

¿Es una ciudad o un buque
en el que fuésemos abandonando la tierra,
callados y felices,
y con tal pureza,
que sólo nuestras almas
en la blancura plenilunar vivieran . . . ?

Y de pronto cruza un vago
estremecimiento por la luz serena.
Las líneas se desvanecen,
la inmensidad cámbiase en blanca piedra,
y sólo permanece en la noche aciaga
la certidumbre de tu ausencia.

at how beautiful the world is
under the age-old full moon's spell.
And the mournful yearning to be loved
flickers in the heavy heart.

There is a city hanging in midair,
a nearly invisible city,
whose hazy outlines
shine through in the clear night.
Its polyhedral crystals form
like watermarks on white paper.
A city so distant
its absurd presence is unsettling.

Is it a city or a ship
in which we'd leave the earth behind,
silent and happy,
so purely
that only our souls
lived on in the full moon's white?

When suddenly a dim shiver
traverses the placid light.
The lines dissolve,
the vast spaces turn to white stone,
and all that remains in the fateful night
is the plain truth of your absence.

Historia de mi muerte

Soñé la muerte y era muy sencillo;

una hebra de seda me envolvía,

y a cada beso tuyo,

con una vuelta menos me ceñía

y cada beso tuyo

era un día;

y el tiempo que mediaba entre dos besos

una noche. La muerte era muy sencilla.

Y poco a poco fue desenvolviéndose

la hebra fatal. Ya no la retenía

sino por solo un cabo entre los dedos ...

Cuando de pronto te pusiste fría

y ya no me besaste ...

y solté el cabo, y se me fue la vida.

Story of My Death

I dreamed of death and it was very simple;
a silken thread wound around me,
and with every kiss from you,
it would unwrap, the less to bind me,
and every one of your kisses
was one day;
and the time between two kisses
was one night. Death was very simple.
And little by little
the fatal thread unraveled. Finally I could only hold on
to the end between my fingers …
When suddenly you went cold
and kissed me no more …
and I let go the end, and my life was gone.

Julio Herrera y Reissig

Like many of his fellow modernistas, the Uruguayan poet Julio Herrera y Reissig (1875–1910) died young—in his case, at thirty-five, of a heart condition. Born into a politically connected family, he worked sporadically as a bureaucrat and published an important political essay in 1902 on the national politics of modernization. In his last years he gathered fellow bohemians in his famous Torre de los Panoramas ("Tower of Panoramas") to build artificial paradises, to recite, and to live the archetypal fin-de-siècle life of the mind. There he proclaimed his independence and would rail at the critics to "¡Dejad en paz a los dioses!" ("Leave the gods alone!"). No one at the time—perhaps anywhere—was writing more hermetic and challenging poetry. He was a kindred spirit to Charles Baudelaire, Arthur Schopenhauer, and Jules Laforgue. His irony—descending often into paroxysms, into pure play of signification—helped turn modernismo fractured, dissonant, nightmarish. Many of his poems tread the line between parody and solemnity so expertly that the reader is caught up in hesitation. Consider Herrera y Reissig's Rimbaudian composition "Solo verde-amarillo para flauta: Llave de U" ("Green-Yellow Solo for Flute: Key of U"), in which almost every word has a long *u* sound, representation ceases to be the goal, and semantics defers entirely to the primacy of sound; or consider "Alba triste" ("Mournful Dawn"), in which he invents the verbs "to epilepsy" and "to Wagner." In "Desolación absurda" ("Absurd Desolation"), he—radically—uses a monorhyme on the first and fourth lines of every stanza. Today the Uruguayan's paternal link to creationism and other avant-garde sensibilities and practices is well understood.

"La vuelta de los campos" ("Return from the Fields") shows an Arcadian side to the poet; "Tertulia lunática" ("Lunatic Gathering") heralds the procedures of the surrealists with their irrational yoking of oneiric images; "Decoración heráldica" ("Heraldic Decoration") makes a ceremony of amorous idealization; "Desolación absurda" ("Absurd Desolation"), an unlikely love poem, gives free reign to the imaginational dimension and the associative powers of language; and "Neurastenia" ("Neurasthenia") conjures a secular mass of sorts.

With the possible exception of Lugones, Herrera y Reissig was the modernista furthest ahead of his time.

La vuelta de los campos

La tarde paga en oro divino las faenas . . .
Se ven limpias mujeres vestidas de percales,
trenzando sus cabellos con tilos y azucenas
o haciendo sus labores de aguja en los umbrales.

Zapatos claveteados y báculos y chales . . .
Dos mozas con sus cántaros se deslizan apenas.
Huye el vuelo sonámbulo de las horas serenas.
Un suspiro de Arcadia peina los matorrales . . .

Cae un silencio austero . . . Del charco que se nimba
estalla una gangosa balada de marimba.
Los lagos se amortiguan con espectrales lampos,

las cumbres, ya quiméricas, corónanse de rosas . . .
Y humean a lo lejos las rutas polvorosas
por donde los labriegos regresan de los campos.

Return from the Fields

The afternoon rewards the toils with divine gold . . .
Clean women dressed in calico,
braiding their hair with linden blossoms and white lilies
or doing their needlework at their doorsteps.

Stud-laced shoes and staffs and shawls . . .
Two maidens with urns slightly tilted.
The sleepwalker's flight flees from the quiet hours.
A sigh from Arcadia combs the thickets . . .

An austere silence falls . . . From the haloed pond
a twangy marimba ballad erupts.
The lakes are silenced by spectral flashes of light,

the peaks, already chimerical, are crowned with roses . . .
And the dusty roads smoke in the distance
where the laborers return from the fields.

(trans. SW)

Tertulia lunática (fragmento)

[*de* La torre de las esfinges: Psicologación morbo-panteísta]

IV

Et noctem quietam concedet dominus . . .

Canta la noche salvaje
sus ventriloquias de Congo,
en un gangoso diptongo
de guturación salvaje . . .
La luna muda su viaje
de astrólogo girasol,
y olímpico caracol,
proverbial de los oráculos,
hunde en el mar sus tentáculos,
hipnotizado de Sol.

Sueña Rodenbach su ambigua
quimera azul, en la bruma;
y el gris surtidor empluma
su frivolidad ambigua . . .
Allá en la mansión antigua,
la noble anciana, de leda
cara de esmalte, remeda
—bajo su crespo algodón—

Lunatic Gathering (excerpt)

[*from* The Tower of the Sphinxes: Morbo-Pantheistic Psychologation]

IV

Et noctem quietam concedet dominus . . .

The savage night sings
its Congo ventriloquism,
a twanging dipthong
made savagely gutteral . . .
The moon transits,
as an astrological sunflower
and an Olympian snail,
proverbial in the oracles,
and sinks its tentacles in the sea,
hypnotized by the sun.

Rodenbach dreams his ambiguous
blue chimaera in the mist;[1]
and the gray fountain plumes
its ambiguous frivolity . . .
Away in the old mansion, her face glowing contented,
the noble old lady—
under her frizzled cotton—

The Latin epigraph means, "And the master acquiesced to the silent night."

[1]George Rodenbach (1855–98) is a Belgian symbolist poet; he is best known for the decadent novel *Bruges-la-morte* (1892).

el copo de una ilusión
envuelto en papel de seda.

En la abstracción de un espejo
introspectivo me copio
y me reitero en mí propio
como en un cóncavo espejo . . .
La sierra nubla un perplejo
rictus de tormenta mómica,
y en su gran página atómica
finge el cielo de estupor
el inmenso borrador
de una música astronómica.

Con insomnios de neuralgia
bosteza el reloj: la una;
y el parque alemán de luna
sufre una blanca neuralgia . . .
Ronca el pino su nostalgia
con latines de arcipreste;
y es el molino una agreste
libélula embalsamada,
en un alfiler picada
a la vitrina celeste.

Un leit-motiv de ultratumba
desarticula el pantano,

imitates a bundle of illusions
wrapped up in silk paper.

In the abstraction of an ingazing looking glass
I copy myself,
and reiterate myself in me
as in a concave mirror . . .
The mountains cloud a perplexed
wince of a mummifying storm,
and on its great atomic page
the great astonished heavens fake
the mammoth first draft
of an astronomical music.

With neuralgic insomnia
the clock yawns: one o'clock;
the German park under moonlight
suffers a white neuralgia . . .
The pine tree snores its nostalgia
with an archpriest's Latin;
the windmill is a wild
embalmed dragonfly,
stuck through with a pin
in the heavenly display case.

A leitmotif from beyond the grave
disjoints the morass,

como un organillo insano
de un carrusel de ultratumba . . .
El Infinito derrumba
su interrogación huraña,
y se suicida, en la extraña
vía láctea, el meteoro,
como un carbunclo de oro
en una tela de araña.

like a crazed barrel organ
of a carousel from the beyond . . .
The Infinite topples
its shy interrogation,
and the meteor takes its own life
in the strange milky way
like a golden carbuncle
in a spider's web.

Decoración heráldica

Señora de mis pobres homenajes.
Débote amar aunque me ultrajes.
—Góngora

Soñé que te encontrabas junto al muro
glacial donde termina la existencia,
paseando tu magnífica opulencia
de doloroso terciopelo obscuro.

Tu pie, decoro del marfil más puro,
hería, con satánica inclemencia,
las pobres almas, llenas de paciencia,
que aún se brindaban a tu amor perjuro.

Mi dulce amor que sigue sin sosiego,
igual que un triste corderito ciego,
la huella perfumada de tu sombra,

buscó el suplicio de tu regio yugo,
y bajo el raso de tu pie verdugo
puse mi esclavo corazón de alfombra.

Heraldic Decoration

Lady of my humble praise.
I must repay with my love your insulting ways.
—*Góngora*

I dreamed you stood by the glacial
wall at the far end of existence,
flourishing your grand opulence
of painful dark velvet.

Your foot, with the propriety of purest ivory,
satanically severe would
spurn the poor souls full of patience
who yet would give themselves in offering to your false love.

My gentle love, which, knowing no peace,
just like a little blind lamb
follows your shadow's scented trail,

sought out the torture of your queenly yoke,
and under your satiny slave driver's foot
for your carpet I lay down my heart enchained.

Desolación absurda (fragmento)

Je serai ton cercueil,
aimable pestilence! . . .

Noche de tenues suspiros
platónicamente ilesos:
vuelan bandadas de besos
y parejas de suspiros;
ebrios de amor, los cefiros
hinchan su leve pulmón,
y los sauces en montón
obseden los camalotes
como torvos hugonotes
de una muda emigración.

Es la divina hora azul
en que cruza el meteoro,
como metáfora de oro
por un gran cerebro azul.
Una encantada Stambul
surge de tu guardapelo,
y llevan su desconsuelo
hacia vagos ostracismos,
floridos sonambulismos
y adioses de terciopelo.

Absurd Desolation (excerpt)

Je serai ton cercueil,
aimable pestilence! . . .

Night of faint sighs

platonically unharmed:

flocks of kisses fly

and pairs of sighs;

drunk on love, the zephyrs

swell their gentle lung,

and the willows en masse

obsess the floating hyacinths

like grim Huguenots

in a silent emigration.

It is the divine blue hour

in which the meteor crosses

like a golden metaphor

through a vast blue brain.

An enchanted Istanbul

emerges from your locket,

and florid somnambulisms

and velvet farewells

carry off their despair

toward vague ostracisms.

The epigraph means, "I will be your casket, kind pestilence! . . ." It comes from Charles Baudelaire's "Le flacon" ("The Perfume Flask").

En este instante de esplín,
mi cerebro es como un piano
donde un aire wagneriano
toca el loco del esplín.
En el lírico festín
de la ontológica altura,
muestra la luna su dura
calavera torva y seca
y hace una rígida mueca
con su mandíbula obscura.

El mar, como gran anciano,
lleno de arrugas y canas,
junto a las playas lejanas
tiene rezongos de anciano.
Hay en acecho una mano
dentro del trembladeral;
y la supersustancial
vía láctea se me finge
la osamenta de una Esfinge
dispersada en un erial.

In this splenetic instant,
my brain is like a piano
on which a man mad with spleen[1]
plays a Wagnerian air.
At the lyrical banquet
in the ontological heights,
the moon reveals her hard, dry
grim skeleton
and grimaces stiffly
with her dark jaw.

The sea, like a grand old man,
full of wrinkles and gray hair,
grouches on far-flung beaches
like an old man.
Within the quaking bog
a hand lies in wait;
and the supersubstantial[2]
Milky Way tries to fool me into thinking
it is the bones of a sphinx
scattered over fallow farmland.

---

[1]Spleen is the seat of ill temper, ennui, and melancholy peculiar to late-nineteenth-century artists, particularly Baudelaire and those in his sway.

[2]*Supersubstantial*: of a transcending substance. The term is used in the context of the Eucharist, the "bread of life." "Give us this day our supersubtantial bread" is the Vulgate translation of *panem supersubstantialem* in Matthew 6.11.

Cantando la tartamuda
frase de oro de una flauta,
recorre el eco su pauta
de música tartamuda.
El entrecejo de Buda
hinca el barranco sombrío,
abre un bostezo de hastío
la perezosa campaña,
y el molino es una araña
que se agita en el vacío.

¡Deja que incline mi frente
en tu frente subjetiva,
en la enferma sensitiva
media luna de tu frente,
que en la copa decadente
de tu pupila profunda
beba el alma vagabunda
que me da ciencias astrales,
en las horas espectrales
de mi vida moribunda!

Deja que rime unos sueños
en tu rostro de gardenia,
Hada de la neurastenia,
trágica luz de mis sueños

Singing the stuttered
golden phrase from a flute,
the echo runs through its score
of stuttering music.
The space between the Buddha's brows
pricks the dark gorge,
the lazy campaign
opens a yawn of boredom,
and the mill is a spider
squirming in the void.

Let my brow rest
on your subjective brow,
on the sick, sensitive
half-moon of your brow,
may the decadent cup
of your profound pupil
drink down the nomadic soul
that gives me astral knowledge
in the spectral hours
of my dying life!

Let me rhyme some dreams
in your gardenia face,
Fairy of neurasthenia,
tragic light of my dreams.

Mercadera de beleños
llévame al mundo que encanta:
soy el genio de Atalanta
que en sus delirios evoca
el ecuador de tu boca
y el polo de tu garganta!

Con el alma hecha pedazos,
tengo un Calvario en el mundo;
amo y soy un moribundo,
tengo el alma hecha pedazos:
cruz me deparan tus brazos,
hiel tus lágrimas salinas,
tus diestras uñas espinas
y dos clavos luminosos
los aleonados y briosos
ojos con que me fascinas!

Oh, mariposa nocturna
de mi lámpara suicida,
alma caduca y torcida,

Trader in henbane,[3]

take me to the enchanting world;

I am the spirit of Atalanta[4]

who in its ravings evokes

the equator of your mouth

and the pole of your throat!

My soul in tatters,

I have a Calvary in the world;

I love and am a dying man,

my soul lies in tatters:

may your arms give me a cross,

bile, your salty tears,

thorns, your skillful fingernails,

and two shining nails

the tawny, lively

eyes with which you bewitch me!

O butterfly of night

in my suicidal lamp,

decrepit, twisted soul,

---

[3]Henbane is a poisonous herb, known variously as fetid nightshade, devil's eye, hebon, hebenon, or belene. It is associated with sleep and stupor. A convulsant, it was used in diabolic rites, prophecy, magic, witches' brews, and love potions. In mythology, the dead wore crowns of henbane in the underworld. Hamlet's father dies after a vial of it is poured in his ear.

[4]Atalanta was a Greek heroine noted for her fleetness of foot. She lost a race with Hippomenes when he distracted her with the golden apples of the Hesperides.

evanescencia nocturna;
linfática taciturna
de mi Nirvana opioso,
en tu mirar sigiloso
me espeluzna tu erotismo
que es la pasión del abismo
por el Ángel Tenebroso!

(Es media noche). Las ranas
torturan en su acordeón
un «piano» de Mendelssohn
que es un gemido de ranas;
habla de cosas lejanas
un clamoreo sutil;
Y con aire acrobatil,
bajo la inquieta laguna,
hace piruetas la luna
sobre una red de marfil.

Juega el viento perfumado,
con los pétalos que arranca,
una partida muy blanca
de un ajedrez perfumado;
pliega el arroyo en el prado
su abanico de cristal,
y genialmente anormal
finge el monte a la distancia

nocturnal evanescence;
O lymphatic moody one
of my opium Nirvana,
in your discreet glance
your erotics—the passion of the abyss
for the Dark Angel!—
send shivers running through me.

(It is midnight.) On their accordion
the frogs are torturing
a Mendelssohn work for piano,
which is the moaning of frogs;
a subtle clamor
talks of far-off things;
with an acrobatic air,
under the troubled lagoon,
the moon does pirouettes
over a net of marble.

The perfumed wind plays
a white, white game
of perfumed chess
with the petals it plucks out;
the creek unfolds in the meadow
its crystal fan,
and kindly abnormal,
the mountain in the distance

una gran protuberancia
del cerebro universal.

Vengo a ti, serpiente de ojos
que hunden crímenes amenos,
la de los siete venenos
en el iris de sus ojos;
beberán tus llantos rojos
mis estertores acerbos,
mientras los fúnebres cuervos,
reyes de las sepulturas,
velan como almas obscuras
de atormentados protervos!

Tú eres póstuma y marchita
misteriosa flor erótica,
miliunanochesca, hipnótica,
flor de Estigia acre y marchita,
tú eres absurda y maldita,
desterrada del Placer,
la paradoja del ser
en el borrón de la Nada,
una hurí desesperada
del harem de Baudelaire!

feigns a giant outgrowth
from the universal mind.

I am coming to you, serpent
with eyes that harbor pleasant crimes,
you of the seven venoms
in the iris of your eyes;
my bitter death rattles
will drink down your red tears,
while the funereal ravens,
kings of the tombs,
stand vigil like the dark tormented shades
of the wicked!

You are posthumous and withered,
a mysterious erotic flower
out of the Arabian Nights, hypnotic,
the pungent, faded flower from the river Styx,
you are absurd and accursed,
outcast from Pleasure,
the paradox of existence
in the smudge of Nothingness,
a desperate houri[5]
from Baudelaire's harem!

[5]A black-eyed virgin from Islamic paradise, the reward of the believer. A houri's virginity is renewable, and she is eternally young and beautiful ("Hou'ri"). Houris appear in Baudelaire's translation of Poe's "Lygeia" and elsewhere.

Ven, reclina tu cabeza
de honda noche delincuente
sobre mi tétrica frente,
sobre mi aciaga cabeza;
deje su indócil rareza
tu numen desolador,
que en el drama inmolador
de nuestros mudos abrazos
yo te abriré con mis brazos
un paréntesis de amor!

Come, lay your head
of deep and evildoing night
against my gloomy brow,
against my ill-fated head;
let your devastating numen
desert its lawless oddity,
for in the immolating drama
of our silent embraces
I will open up for you
parentheses of love with my arms!

Neurastenia

Le spectre de la réalite
traverse ma pensée.
—*Victor Hugo*

Huraño el bosque muge su rezongo,
y los ecos llevando algún reproche
hacen rodar su carrasqueño coche
y hablan la lengua de un extraño Congo.

Con la expresión estúpida de un hongo,
clavado en la ignorancia de la noche,
muere la Luna. El humo hace un fantoche
de pies de sátiro y sombrero oblongo.

Híncate! Voy a celebrar la misa.
Bajo la azul genuflexión de Urano
adoraré cual hostia tu camisa:

"¡Oh, tus botas, los guantes, el corpiño . . . !"
Tu seno expresará sobre mi mano
la metempsícosis de un astro niño.

Neurasthenia

Le spectre de la réalité
traverse ma pensée.
—*Victor Hugo*

Reticently the woods groan and grumble,
their echoes carrying some complaint
like an oaken car rolling roughly along,
speaking in the tongue of some strange Congo.

With a mushroom's stupid expression,
nailed in the ignorance of night,
the Moon dies. The smoke draws a marionette
with satyr feet and an oblong hat.

Kneel down! I will now celebrate Mass.
Beneath the blue genuflection of Uranus
I will adore your blouse as if it were a host:

"Oh, your boots, your gloves, your brassiere . . . !"
Your bosom will impress upon my hand
the metempsychosis of a baby star.

(*trans. SW*)

The epigraph means, "The specter of reality pierces my thoughts."

María Eugenia Vaz Ferreira

Uruguayan poet and friend of Delmira Agustini, both part of the Generación del 1900 ("Generation of 1900"), María Eugenia Vaz Ferreira (1875–1924) might have become as great as her younger contemporary had she not succumbed to madness in her prime. Her brother Carlos, an important man of letters, undertook to organize and publish her most essential texts in *La isla de los cánticos* (1924; "The Isle of Songs"), when María Eugenia's health was failing. She was anthologized often in the early twentieth century, notably in Juan Parra del Riego's *Antología de poetisas americanas* (1923) and Tílda Brito de Donoso's *Poetisas de América* (1929), and recently she appeared in Manuel Francisco Reina's *Mujeres de carne y verso: Antología poética femenina en lengua española del siglo XX* (2002). Among her best compositions are "El regreso" (1924; The Return; or, Homecoming) and "El ataúd flotante" (1921; "The Floating Coffin"). Below we present the first known translations of her poetry into English, and she will be new even to many who are familiar with works from the era.

Our selection features "Rendición" ("Surrender"; in Spanish it is also known as "Holocausto" ["Burnt Offering"]), a poem that may be an ironic response to Díaz Mirón's "A Gloria" (a play on "To Glory" and "To Gloria"), the last lines of which are:

Confórmate, mujer! Hemos venido
a este valle de lágrimas que abate,
tú, como la paloma, para el nido,
y yo, como el león, para el combate. (314)

Fall in line, woman! We have come
to this dispiriting vale of tears,
you, like the dove, for the nest,
and I, like the lion, for the fight.

"Yo sola" ("I Alone") has an unexpected twist. "Los desterrados" ("The Exiles") is an atmospheric poem of a woman's longing.

A major international poetry prize in Uruguay today bears Vaz Ferreira's name.

Rendición

Quebrantaré en tu honra mi vieja rebeldía
si sabe combatirme la ciencia de tu mano,
si tienes la grandeza de un templo soberano
ofrendaré mi sangre para tu idolatría.
Naufragará en tus brazos la prepotencia mía
si tienes la profunda fruición del océano
y si sabes el ritmo de un canto sobrehumano
silenciarán mis arpas su eterna melodía.

Me volveré paloma si tu soberbia siente
la garra vencedora del águila potente:
si sabes ser fecundo seré tu floración,
y brotaré una selva de cósmicas entrañas,
cuyas salvajes frondas románticas y hurañas
conquistará tu imperio si sabes ser león.

Surrender

In your honor I will break my rebellion of old
if your hand's skill can battle me;
if you have the grandeur of a sovereign temple,
for your idolatry I will offer up my blood.
My dominance will founder in your arms
if you possess the deep delight of the sea,
and if you know the rhythm of a superhuman song,
my harps will silence their eternal melody.

I will become a dove if your haughtiness feels
the conquering talon of the mighty eagle:
if you can be fruitful, I will be your flowering,
and I will bring forth a jungle of cosmic feeling,
whose shy and wild romantic leaves
shall overcome your kingdom, if you can be a lion.

Yo sola

Quisiera circundarte de serpientes
ungidas de mortíferas ponzoñas;
infiltrarte maléficos perfumes,
encrespar junto a ti pérfidas olas.
Colgarte encima trémulas campanas
de bronce rudo, cuya voz sonora
vertiginosamente el aire atruene
con el eco tonante de sus glosas . . .
Cavarte al pie siniestras sepulturas
abriendo sin cesar trágicas bocas;
suspender sobre ti fúlgidas hachas,
raudos puñales y tajantes hojas . . .
Posar sobre tus hombros, cuervos, buhos,
vampiros y lechuzas pavorosas,
que soplen en el aire que te cerca
el vaho helado de sus alas lóbregas . . .
desatar polvaredas, remolinos,
rachas de tempestad, hórridas trombas,
rayos, piras, volcanes, mares, vientos
de salvaje potencia arrolladora,
y arrollarte en una gran mortaja
para que nunca, nunca, nunca, otra
se acerque a ti!

I Alone

I would like to surround you with serpents
anointed with deadly fangs;
to infiltrate you with evil perfumes,
to whip up treacherous waves around you.
To hang quivering bells above you
made of crude bronze, whose ringing sounds
dizzily deafen the air
with the thundering echo of their tongues . . .
To dig dark graves at your feet
that open tragic mouths without end;
to poise radiant axes over you,
swift knives and cutting blades . . .
To set crows, eagle owls, vampire bats,
and dreadful owls on your shoulders
to exhale in the wind that besieges you
the chill reek of their gloomy wings . . .
To unleash dust clouds, whirlwinds,
storm squalls, horrendous tornadoes,
bolts of lightning, funeral pyres, volcanoes, seas, winds
of wild consuming power,
and to roll you up in a giant shroud
so that no other woman can come near you,
ever, ever, ever.

Los desterrados

Una fría tarde triste
yendo por una apartada
ruta, al través de los turbios
cristales de una ventana
yo lo vi gallardamente
curvado sobre las fraguas.
El cabello sudoroso
en ondas le negreaba
chorreando salud y fuerza
sobre la desnuda espalda.
Le relucían los ojos
y la boca le brillaba
henchida de sangre roja
bajo la ceniza parda.
Y era el acre olor del hierro
luz de chispas incendiarias,
rudo golpe del martillo,
vaho ardiente de las ascuas,
que las mal justas rendijas
hasta mí fluir dejaban
con ecos de cosa fuerte
y efluvios de cosa sana.
«Dios de las misericordias
que los destinos amparas,
cuando me echaste a la vida

The Exiles

Of an evening sad and cold
traveling down a distant
trail, through cloudy
windowpanes
I saw him poised, bent gracefully
over the forge.
His hair, running with sweat,
blackened him in waves
gushing health and power
all down his bare back.
His eyes sparkled
and his mouth shone
brimming full of red blood
under the dark ash.
And it was the bitter smell of steel
the light of fiery sparks,
the hard clang of the hammer,
the hot steam of the live coals
that the tiny openings
sent flowing to me
in echoes of something strong
and exhalations of vitality.
"Merciful God,
refuge for our lives,
when you cast me into life,

¿por qué me pusiste un alma?
Mírame como Ahasvero
siempre triste y solitaria,
soñando con las quimeras
y las divinas palabras . . .
Mírame por mi camino,
como por una vía apia
de sonrisas incoloras
y de vacías miradas . . .
¿Por qué no te plugo hacerme
libre de secretas ansias,
como a la feliz doncella
que esta noche y otras tantas
en el hueco de esos brazos
hallará la suma gracia?»
Así me quejé y a poco
seguí la tediosa marcha,
arropada entre las brumas
pluviosas, y me obsediaban
como brazos extendidos
los penachos de las llamas

why did you give me a soul?

Look upon me as you would Ahasuerus,[1]

forever sad and lonely,

dreaming of castles in the air

and of words sublime . . .

Look upon me on my journey,

as if down an Appian Way[2]

of lifeless smiles

and vacant stares . . .

Why was it not your will

to free me of these secret pangs of yearning

like the blessed girl

who tonight, like so many other nights,

will find the supreme grace

in the hollow of his open arms?"

This was my plaint, and not long after

I rejoined my wearisome course,

wrapped in rainy mists,

obsessed

by what seemed the outstretched arms

of the plumes of smoke from the flames

---

[1]Ahasuerus is the Wandering Jew, the legendary undying penitent forced to wander the earth until Judgment Day for mistreatment of Jesus on the way to Calvary.

[2]A famous road in ancient Rome, built in 312 BCE. Thousands of slaves were crucified there, including the followers of Spartacus's rebellion in 71 BCE.

y unos ojos relucientes

adonde se reflejaba

el dorado y luminoso

serpenteo de las fraguas.

and a pair of gleaming eyes in which
the luminous twisting gold
rising from the forge
was shining out.

José Santos Chocano

José Santos Chocano (1875–1934) has often been associated with the *mundonovista* phase of modernismo: a heroic poetry that vigorously championed autochthonous—Americanist—values, style, and imagery. Rhetorical and epic in scope, the Peruvian's expansive poetry bears the impress of a pervasive, inflated *yo poético*, or first-person narrator, a persona that claimed the dual identity of Hispanic and pre-Columbian, praising both the exploited Indian and the exploits of the conquistadors. At times recalling José Eustasio Rivera's 1921 collection of Parnassian sonnets of the jungle, *Tierra de Promisión* ("Promised Land"), the modernista sensibility applied to wild nature in Santos Chocano's work made for some unique poetic conceits. From his earliest important work—*Iras santas* (1893–95; "Holy Fury"), printed in red ink—the civic bard assumes the insistent voice of national redeemer and opposer of tyrants (69–96). During the Mexican Revolution the poet collaborated with Pancho Villa, to whom he dedicated his poem "Última rebelión" (156; "Final Revolt"). Styling himself an heir to the discoverers, Santos Chocano sought to represent the American continent—geography, race, history, the *cornucopia americana*, as Pablo Neruda would in *Canto general* in 1950. Walt Whitman was an obvious inspiration for this poetic enterprise, though with a significant divergence, as José Olivio Jiménez notes: Whitman looked to the dynamic future, Santos Chocano to the frozen past (420).

"Blasón" ("Coat of Arms"), "Los volcanes" ("The Volcanos"), and "Oda salvaje" ("Wild Ode") are among his most representative and anthologized poems; *Alma América* (1906; "Soul of the Americas") is his most popular collection. Santos Chocano was featured in the prestigious *Poetry* magazine in 1918.

Here we offer "Las orquídeas" ("Orchids"), in which the prized flower seeks the heights away from the warring elements below; and the aforementioned "Oda salvaje" ("Wild Ode"), a time-traveling, panoptic epic. "Wild" (the Spanish also connotes "savage") describes the work's loose metrics as well.

After a life of contentious economic dealings, Santos Chocano was stabbed to death on a streetcar by a Chilean worker who felt he had been wronged by him.

Las orquídeas

Caprichos de cristal, airosas galas
de enigmáticas formas sorprendentes,
diademas propias de apolíneas frentes
adornos dignos de fastuosas salas.

En los nudos de un tronco hacen escalas;
y ensortijan sus tallos de serpientes,
hasta quedar en la altitud pendientes,
a manera de pájaros sin alas.

Tristes como cabezas pensativas,
brotan ellas, sin torpes ligaduras
de tirana raíz, libres y altivas;

porque también, con lo mezquino en guerra,
quieren vivir, como las almas puras,
sin un solo contacto con la tierra . . .

Orchids

Whims of glass, graceful jewels
of startling, enigmatic forms,
diadems for Appolonian brows,
adornments worthy of opulent sitting rooms.

In the knots of tree trunks they make rope ladders,
snaking their stems skyward
until hanging from the heights
like wingless birds.

Sad as heads deep in thought
they bloom, free and proud,
without ungainly bonds of tyrannical root;

for, while the poor in spirit are at war,
orchids wish to live, akin to purest souls,
without a single contact with the earth . . .

Oda salvaje (fragmentos)

Selva de mis abuelos primitivos,
diosa tutelar de los Incas y de los Aztecas,
yo te saludo, desde el mar, que estremece
todas sus espumas para besarte, como besa
un viejo esclavo
los pies de su Reina;
yo te saludo, desde el mar, sobre cuyas crines
tus brisas perfumadas se restriegan
y tus troncos mutilados
señalan a la aventura el camino de las Américas;
yo te saludo, desde el mar, que es amable
como un cacique de intonsa cabellera
y que sabe que de los apretados renglones
de tu indescrifrable leyenda
sale el árbol hueco y alígero
que lo muerde con la quilla y lo devora con la vela;
yo te saludo, selva de mis abuelos primitivos,
diosa tutelar de los Incas y de los Aztecas . . .

Vuelvo a ti sano del alma,
a pesar de las civilizaciones enfermas:
tu vista me conforta,
porque al verte, me siento a la manera
de los viejos caciques,
que dormían sobre la yerba
y bebían leche de cabras salvajes

Wild Ode (excerpts)

Forest of my early forefathers,
tutelary goddess of the Incas and the Aztecs,
I salute you from the sea whose spindrift
trembles to kiss you,
as an old slave kisses
the feet of his Queen;
I salute you from the sea, over whose mane
your scented breezes brush
and your mutilated logs
point the way to the adventure of the Americas;
I salute you from the sea, which is kind
like a long-haired Indian chief
and which knows that from the crowded lines
of your indecipherable legend
comes the hollow, shortened tree
that nibbles at it with its keel and gulps it with its sail;
I salute you, forest of my early forefathers,
tutelary goddess of the Incas and the Aztecs . . .

I return to you healthy of soul,
despite the sick civilizations:
the sight of you comforts me,
for when I see you I feel as
the old Indian chiefs felt,
they who slept on the grass
and drank the milk of wild goats

y comían pan de maíz con miel de abejas;
tu vista me conforta,
porque tu espesura de ejército me recuerda
de cuando, hace novecientos años,
discurrí a la cabeza
de veinte mil arqueros bravíos,
que, arrancándose del éxodo tolteca
fueron hasta el país de los lagos y de los volcanes,
en donde el chontal sólo se rindió ante la Reina,
y de cuando trasmigré al imperio armonioso
del gran Inca Yupanqui, y le seguí, por las sierras
a las vertientes de Arauco,
en donde con alas de cóndor nos improvisábamos tiendas;
tu vista me conforta,
porque sé que los siglos me señalan como tu Poeta,
y recojo, del fondo alucinante
de tus edades quiméricas,

and ate corn bread with honey;

the sight of you comforts me,

for your thicket-like legions of soldiers bring to mind

the time, nine hundred years ago,

I led a thousand fierce bowmen,

who, escaping in the exodus of the Toltecs,[1]

went to the land of lakes and volcanoes,

where the Chontal Indians[2] only surrendered to the Queen,

and from where I transmigrated to the harmonic empire

of the great Inca Yupanqui,[3] and I followed him through the mountains

to the slopes of Arauco,[4]

where with condor wings we rigged up makeshift tents;

the sight of you comforts me,

for I know that the centuries appoint me your Poet,

and I gather from the dreamlike depths

of your fantastic ages

---

[1]"[T]he Nahuatl-speaking Toltecs began moving east towards Nicaragua from the ninth century onwards, in part because of pressure exerted by the 'barbarian' Chichimec" (Brotherston 167n32).

[2]*Chontales* was the name the Spanish gave the Mayan people of Oaxaca, Mexico; the term derives from the Aztec *chontalli* ("foreigner").

[3]Pachacuti Inca Yupanqui (1438–71), also known as Pachacutec, was an expansionist emperor of the Incas and master administrator of conquered tribes. He oversaw the construction of the major monuments of the Inca empire, including the Temple of the Sun, Sacsahuaman, and Machu Picchu.

[4]Arauco is a region of Chile south of the Bío Bío River. The *Araucana* is a sixteenth-century masterpiece of Spanish epic poetry by Alonso de Ercilla; it tells of the heroic battle of the Spanish against the Araucanians, a Chilean tribe who call themselves Mapuches.

la voz con que se dolían y exaltaban,
en sus liras de piedra,
los haraviccus del Cuzco
y los Emperadores Aztecas.

Tuya es la danta
que sorprende en los charcos la deformidad de su silueta
y se va abriendo paso, entre los matorrales,
al golpe enérgico de su cabeza:
tuyo el jaguar, que brinca,
en el alarde acrobático de sus fuerzas,
a los árboles corpulentos
para dejarse caer súbito sobre su presa;
tuyo el tigrillo, que urde
taimadas estrategias,
para los carnívoros alborozos
de sus dientes de alabastro y sus encías de felpa;
tuyo el lagarto, dios anfibio y vetusto,
que preside las lluvias y las siembras
y condecora con las esmeraldas de sus ojos
las taciturnas oquedades de las cuevas;
tuyo el boa,
que se dijera

the voice with which
the haraviccus of Cuzco[5]
and the Aztec emperors
grieved and praised
on their lyres of stone.

Yours is the tapir
startled by its own misshapen shadow in the ponds
and who rams his way
headlong through the thicket:
yours the jaguar, who leaps,
in an acrobatic display of its might,
into the thick-trunked trees,
then pounces down on its prey;
yours the wildcat who hatches
sly plots
for the carnivorous delight
of his alabaster teeth and his gums of plush;
yours the alligator, an amphibious and ancient god,
who rules over the rains and the sowing season
and decorates the dour and hollow spaces of the caves
with the emeralds of its eyes;
yours the boa,
whom one would think

[5]Poet-historians of the Inca; they are described in book 19 of Inca Garcilaso de la Vega's *Comentarios reales*.

un brazo interminable
recortado a las sombras por un hacha dantesca . . .

. . . .

Ahora que a ti retorno
y me siento con tu savia en las venas,
creo desenterrar los siglos
y hacerlos desfilar por tu juventud perpetua:
evoco yo los tiempos obscuros
en que tu primer árbol cuajó sobre una piedra
y apareciéronte todos de repente,
aquí y allá, con el ordenado desorden de las estrellas;
y evoco yo los tiempos sucesivos
que han pasado en una procesión monótona y lenta,
hasta que tus raíces succionaron el ímpetu,
y tus troncos se acorazaron en sus cortezas,
y los nudos de tus ramas se desataron
en este himno inacabable de tu única Primavera.
Jaula florida de pájaros sinfónicos,
eres como el fantasma de una orquesta:
sinsontes y turpiales
ponen en tus oídos estupefactos músicas nuevas;
y solamente mudo
el quetzal heráldico te ornamenta,

an unending arm

chopped off in the darkness by a Dantean ax . . .

. . . .

Now that I return to you

and feel your life force in my veins,

I feel I am unearthing the centuries

and over your eternal youth I make them file past:

I conjure the dim age

in which your first tree took hold on a rock

and all of them appeared to you at once,

scattered with the ordered disorder of the stars;

and in a slow, monotonous procession,

I call up age after age that has gone before,

until your roots soaked up the momentum,

and your trunks hardened in their bark,

and the gnarls of your branches untangled

into this hymn everlasting of your only spring.

Flowered cage of symphonic birds,

you are like the ghost in an orchestra:

centzontli birds and tupials[6]

fill your thunderstruck ears with new songs;

and merely silent,

the heraldic quetzal[7] decorates you,

---

[6]*Centzontli* or *tzenzontle* is Nahuatl for "bird with four hundred [myriad] songs." The tupial is a native songbird.

[7]A sacred bird of ancient Mesoamerica, the quetzal is highly prized for its iridescent feathers.

arcoirisando el símbolo de sus largas plumas
sobre las sienes de una gran raza muerta . . .

Tus mariposas azules y rosadas
se abanican como damas coquetas;
tus cantáridas brillan
como las talismánicas piedras
incrustadas en las empuñaduras
de las espadas viejas:
tus chicharras se hinchan clamorosas
en una fiebre de pitonisas coléricas;
y en la pesadilla
de tus noctámbulas tinieblas,
se confunde
el pestañeo de las luciérnagas
con el temblor azufrado
de las pupilas satánticas de las fieras . . .

Selva de mis abuelos primitivos,
diosa tutelar de los Incas y de los Aztecas,
yo te saludo, desde el mar; y te pido
que en la noche—en la noche que está cerca—
me sepultes
en tus tinieblas,

rainbowing its long-feathered symbol
across the brow of a great dead race . . .

Your pink and blue butterflies
fan themselves like coquettes;
your cantharides[8] shine
like the talismanic stones
inlaid in the hilts
of ancient swords:
your cicadas swell,
a fevered din of angry soothsayers;
and in the nightmare
of your prowling dark, the blinking
of the fireflies
mingles
with the brimstone temblor
of the satanic eyes of wild beasts . . .

Forest of my early forefathers,
tutelary goddess of the Incas and the Aztecs,
I salute you from the sea; and I ask
that in the night—in the night that's drawing near—
you bury me
in your dark shadows,

---

[8]Cantharis or cantharides is the blue-green blister beetle used in the medical preparation known as Spanish fly.

como si me creyeses un fantasma

de tus religiones muertas,

y me brindes, para salvajizar mis ojos

con reverberaciones de fiesta,

en la punta de cada uno de tus árboles

ensartada una estrella.

as if you believed me a ghost
of your dead religions,
and that you offer me, to make my eyes wild
with the ringing echo of festivities,
a star snagged on the tip
of each of your trees.

Juana Borrero

Mythified by her uncommon talent for both painting and poetry, her disdain for the lowly pursuits of the common run, and her spiritual affinity with Julián del Casal, whom she idolized but who loved her only like a brother (Casal died in 1893, a hard loss for the sensitive girl), the Cuban Juana Borrero (1877–96) nevertheless has been denied her place in turn-of-the-century letters. Borrero came from a family of writers, including Dulce María Borrero, and according to Sidonia Carmen Rosenbaum she was related on her mother's side to the great Gertrudis Gómez de Avellaneda (46). The "adolescente atormentada" ("tortured adolescent"), as she was known (see Augier), was only eighteen when she fell ill and died in exile in Key West, the while lamenting her absent fiancé, Carlos Pio Uhrbach. María Elena de Valdés notes that nearly two volumes of effusive letters to Uhrbach—one of them even written in Borrero's own blood—were collected and published one hundred years after her death (323). Rubén Darío judged the Cuban's poems, many of them sonnets, to be filled with a "very strange, mystic sensuality" (Monner Sans 253).

Here we feature "Apolo" ("Apollo"), which presents an uncommon trope: a woman embracing a male statue with a Pygmalion longing to bring it to life. "Las hijas de Ran" ("The Daughters of Ran") alludes to the nine billows—the undines (wave maidens or water spirits) of Scandinavian myth; their mother, Ran, was queen of the sea and patroness of unmarried girls. "Íntima" ("Intimate") explores the private space of grief.

In *Bustos y rimas* (1892; "Busts and Rhymes"), Julián del Casal dedicated "Marina" to her; his "Juana Borrero" evokes a heart-heavy and precocious girl whose heart was a "negra mariposa / en fragante margarita"("black butterfly / in a fragrant daisy") (290). Borrero has been eulogized by the great masters, from Rubén Darío to Cintio Vitier, though none with so immortal a tribute as one from Casal himself, the 1893 silhouette "Virgen triste" ("Sad Virgin"), a poem that is still admired; in it, she is "de esas castas visiones / que teniendo nostalgia de otras regiones, / ansían de la tierra volar muy lejos" ("one of those chaste visions / that with nostalgia of other regions / yearn to fly far away"). Casal always saw in her "la tristeza / de los seres que deben morir temprano" ("the sadness / of those who must die young") (352).

Apolo

Marmóreo, altivo, refulgente y bello,
corona de su rostro la dulzura,
cayendo en torno de su frente pura
en ondulados rizos sus cabellos.

Al enlazar mis brazos a su cuello
y al estrechar su espléndida hermosura,
anhelante de dicha y de ventura
la blanca frente con mis labios sello.

Contra su pecho inmóvil, apretada
adoré su belleza indiferente,
y al quererla animar, desesperada,

llevada por mi amante desvarío,
dejé mil besos de ternura ardiente
allí apagados sobre el mármol frío.

Apollo

marble

Marmoreal and proud, resplendent, beautiful,
tenderness crowned his face,
his locks falling over his pure brow
in wavy curls.

As I wrapped my arms around his neck
and held his magnificent beauty tight,
longing for bliss, for happiness,
I pressed my lips to his white forehead.

Pulled close against his unmoving breast
I worshipped his indifferent beauty,
wanting desperately to give it life,

carried away by my raving love,
I planted a thousand tender, burning kisses
that by the marble's chill were doused.

* ekphrasis – verse that describes a visual work of art

Las hijas de Ran

Envueltas entre espumas diamantinas
que salpican sus cuerpos sonrosados,
por los rayos del sol iluminados,
surgen del mar en grupo las ondinas.

Cubriendo sus espaldas peregrinas
descienden los cabellos destrenzados,
y al rumor de las olas van mezclados
los ecos de sus risas argentinas.

Así viven contentas y dichosas
entre el cielo y el mar, regocijadas,
ignorando tal vez que son hermosas,

Y que las olas, entre sí rivales,
se entrechocan, de espuma coronadas,
por estrechar sus formas virginales.

The Daughters of Ran

Girdled in diamantine foam
that sprays their blushing bodies
lit up by the rays of the sun,
the undines arise as one from the sea.

All down their wandering backs
their unbraided tresses fall,
and the murmur of the waves is mingled
with the echo of their silver laugh.

Their life is happy and is bliss,
overjoyed are they between the sky and sea,
unaware, perhaps, of how beautiful they are,

and that the rivaling waves
collide, foam-crested, one against the other,
to take their virgin forms in tight embrace.

Íntima

¿Quieres sondear la noche de mi espíritu?

Allá en el fondo oscuro de mi alma

hay un lugar donde jamás penetra

la clara luz del sol de la esperanza.

¡Pero no me preguntes lo que duerme

bajo el sudario de la sombra muda . . .

detente allí junto al abismo, y llora

como se llora al borde de las tumbas!

Intimate

Do you want to plumb the night of my spirit?

Down in the dark depths of my soul

there is a place where never

does the bright sunlight of hope break in.

But don't ask me what is sleeping

under the shroud of the silent shade . . .

stop there at the abyss's edge, and weep

as one weeps beside the tomb!

Delmira Agustini

A daughter of privilege, the Uruguayan poet Delmira Agustini (1886–1914) wrote transgressive verse against the prevailing patriarchy of turn-of-the-century Montevideo, which naturally was ill at ease with her and her work. Her rebellious evocations of female desire, mystic-erotic union, and frustration take surreal turns, employing startling, proliferating metaphors that underscore the violence of her passion. Witness her poem "Visión" ("Vision"), in which the lover is addressed thus: "apareciste / como un hongo gigante, muerto y vivo" ("you appeared / like a giant mushroom, dead and alive") (288). Her choice of images distanced her work from the commonplace modernista appurtenances into an imagery of pain, corrosion, and creatures of night and nightmare. Eros and Thanatos meet frequently in her verses. Disillusionment—with undercurrents of indignation at betrayal—is a dominant tone throughout her poetry. In "Tu amor . . ." ("Your love . . ."), for instance, the narrator accuses her man:

> Pico de cuervo con olor de rosas,
> aguijón enmelado de delicias
> tu lengua es. Tus manos misteriosas
> son garras enguantadas de caricias. (349)

> A crow's beak smelling of roses,
> a honeyed thorn of delights
> your tongue is. Your mysterious hands
> are gloved claws of caresses.

"El intruso" ("The Intruder") is a frank treatment of sexuality from a woman's perspective. "Las alas" ("The Wings") provides a dynamic fantasy of empowerment and freedom. "Lo inefable" ("The Ineffable") treats of the angst of creation. "Nocturno" ("Nocturnal") poetically reimagines the *reino interior* or kingdom within. "El cisne" ("The Swan"), full of imagistic transformations, offers a fine example of the writer's intensity. And "Nocturno" ("Nocturne") is a revealing companion piece to other, more classical treatments of the swan in the modernista canon.

Agustini came under the sway of Rubén Darío himself, who championed her work. She was instrumental to subsequent generations of Latin American women writers in particular, who saw her as a foremother. She was killed by her estranged husband in a fit of jealousy.

El intruso

Amor, la noche estaba trágica y sollozante
cuando tu llave de oro cantó en mi cerradura;
luego, la puerta abierta sobre la sombra helante
tu sombra fue una mancha de amor y de blancura.

Todo aquí lo alumbraron tus ojos de diamante;
bebieron en mi copa tus labios de frescura,
y descansó en mi almohada tu cabeza fragante;
me encantó tu descaro y adoré tu locura.

¡Y hoy río si tú ríes, y canto si tú cantas;
Y si tú duermes, duermo como un perro a tus plantas!
¡Hoy llevo hasta en mi sombra tu olor a primavera;
y tiemblo si tu mano toca la cerradura
y bendigo la noche sollozante y oscura
que floreció en mi vida tu boca tempranera!

The Intruder

Love, the night was tragic and sobbing
when your gold key sang in my lock;
then, the door open upon the freezing shadows,
your shape a stain of light and whiteness.

Your diamond eyes shone upon everything here;
your cool lips drank from my cup;
and on my pillow your fragrant head did rest;
I loved your brazenness, adored your madness.

And today I laugh when you laugh, and sing when you sing;
and when you sleep, like a dog I sleep at your feet!
Today even my shadow carries the smell of your spring;

And I tremble if your hand touches the lock;
and bless the sobbing and dark night
that your early mouth bloomed into my life!

(trans. SW)

Las alas

. . . .

Yo tenía . . .

¡dos alas! . . .

¡Dos alas,
que del Azur vivían como dos siderales
raíces! . . .
Dos alas,
con todos los milagros de la vida, la Muerte
y la ilusión. Dos alas,
fulmíneas
como el velamen de una estrella en fuga;
dos alas,
como dos firmamentos
con tormentas, con calmas y con astros . . .

¿Te acuerdas de la gloria de mis alas? . . .
El áureo campaneo
del ritmo; el inefable
matiz atesorando
el Iris todo, mas un Iris nuevo
ofuscante y divino,
que adorarán las plenas pupilas del Futuro
(Las pupilas maduras a toda luz! . . .) el vuelo . . .

El vuelo ardiente, devorante y único,
que largo tiempo atormentó los cielos,
despertó soles, bólidos, tormentas,

The Wings

. . . .

I used to have . . .

two wings! . . .

Two wings,
living off the Azure like two roots in
space! . . .
Two wings,
with all the miracles of life, Death
and illusion. Two wings,
incandescent
like the canvas of a star in flight;
two wings,
like two firmaments
like storms, with calm and stars . . .

Do you recall the glory of my wings? . . .
The rhythm
of their aureate tolling; the ineffable
hue filling
the entire Iris, but a new Iris
obfuscating and divine,
adoring the full pupils of the Future
(Pupils mature in full light! . . .) the flight . . .

The burning flight, devouring and unique,
which long tormented the heavens,
awoke suns, large meteors, storms,

abrillantó los rayos y los astros;

y la amplitud: tenían

calor y sombra para todo el Mundo,

y hasta incubar un *más allá* pudieron.

Un día, raramente

desmayada a la tierra,

yo me adormí en las felpas profundas de este bosque . . .

Soñé divinas cosas! . . .

Una sonrisa tuya me despertó, paréceme . . .

Y no siento mis alas! . . .

Mis alas? . . .

—Yo las *vi* deshacerse entre mis brazos . . .

¡Era como un deshielo!

lighted the rays and the stars;

and their amplitude: enough

heat and shade for the entire World,

that even of incubating a *beyond* were they capable.

One day, strangely

fainted upon the earth,

I fell here asleep on the deep plush of the forest . . .

I had divine dreams! . . .

A smile of yours awoke me, I think . . .

And I did not feel my wings! . . .

My wings? . . .

—I *saw* them dissolving in my arms . . .

As if something were melting!

(trans. SW)

Lo inefable

Yo muero extrañamente . . . No me mata la Vida,
no me mata la Muerte, no me mata el Amor;
muero de un pensamiento mudo como una herida . . .
¿No habéis sentido nunca el extraño dolor

de un pensamiento inmenso que se arraiga en la vida,
devorando alma y carne, y no alcanza a dar flor?
¿Nunca llevasteis dentro una estrella dormida
que os abrasaba enteros y no daba un fulgor? . . .

Cumbre de los Martirios! . . . Llevar eternamente,
desgarradora y árida, la trágica simiente
clavada en las entrañas como un diente feroz! . . .

Pero arrancarla un día en una flor que abriera
milagrosa, inviolable! . . . Ah, más grande no fuera
tener entre las manos la cabeza de Dios!

The Ineffable

I die a strange death . . . It is not Life that kills me.

It is not Death that kills me, it is not Love that kills me.

I die of an unuttered thought like a wound . . .

Have you never felt the strange pain

of a giant thought that takes root in life,

devouring soul and flesh, and cannot quite flower?

Have you never borne inside you a dormant star

that roasted you whole and gave no light? . . .

Summit of martyrdoms! . . . To bear for all eternity

the tragic seed, heart-rending and arid,

driven into your insides like a terrible tooth! . . .

But to yank it out one day as a flower blooming

miraculous, inviolable! . . . Ah, it would be no greater

to have the head of God in your hands!

Nocturno

Fuera, la noche en veste de tragedia solloza
como una enorme viuda pegada a mis cristales.

Mi cuarto: . . .
por un bello milagro de la luz y del fuego
mi cuarto es una gruta de oro y gemas raras:
tiene un musgo tan suave, tan hondo de tapices,
y es tan vívida y cálida, tan dulce que me creo
dentro de un corazón . . .

Mi lecho que está en blanco es blanco y vaporoso
como flor de inocencia,
como espuma de vicio!
        Esta noche hace insomnio;
hay noches negras, negras, que llevan en la frente
una rosa de sol . . .
En estas noches negras y claras no se duerme.

Y yo te amo, Invierno!
Yo te imagino viejo,
yo te imagino sabio,
con un divino cuerpo de mármol palpitante
que arrastra como un manto regio el peso del Tiempo . . .

Nocturnal

Outside, the night sobs in tragic garments:
an enormous widow against my window.

My room: . . .
by a beautiful miracle of light and fire
my room is a grotto of gold and rare gems:
It has such soft moss, is so deep with tapestries,
and so vivid and warm, so sweet that I believe myself
inside a heart . . .

My bed in white is white and airy
like a flower of innocence,
like the foam of vice!
        Tonight there is insomnia;
there are dark, dark nights, wearing sun-roses
on their foreheads . . .
On these dark and clear nights there is no sleep.

And I love you, Winter!
I imagine you old,
I imagine you wise,
with a divine body of beating marble
dragging the weight of Time like a regal gown . . .

Invierno, yo te amo y soy la primavera . . .
Yo sonroso, tú nievas:
tú porque todo sabes,
yo porque todo sueño . . .

. . . Amémonos por eso! . . .
Sobre mi lecho en blanco,
tan blanco y vaporoso como flor de inocencia,
como espuma de vicio,
Invierno, invierno, invierno,
caigamos en un ramo de rosas y de lirios!

Winter, I love you and I am springtime . . .

I blush, you snow;

you because you know all,

I because I dream all . . .

. . . Let us love each other because of this! . . .

On my white bed,

as white and airy as a flower of innocence,

like the foam of vice,

Winter, Winter, Winter,

let us fall on a bouquet of roses and lilies!

(trans. SW)

El cisne

Pupila azul de mi parque
es el sensitivo espejo
de un lago claro, muy claro! . . .
Tan claro que a veces creo
que en su cristalina página
se imprime mi pensamiento.

Flor del aire, flor del agua,
alma del lago es un cisne
con dos pupilas humanas,
grave y gentil como un príncipe;
alas lirio, remos rosa . . .
Pico en fuego, cuello triste
y orgulloso, y la blancura
y la suavidad de un cisne . . .

El ave cándida y grave
tiene un maléfico encanto;
—clavel vestido de lirio,
trasciende a llama y milagro! . . .
Sus alas blancas me turban
como dos cálidos brazos;
ningunos labios ardieron
como su pico en mis manos,
ninguna testa ha caído
tan lánguida en mi regazo;

The Swan

The blue pupil of my park
is the sensitive looking glass
of a clear—a very clear!—lake . . .
So clear I sometimes believe
my thoughts are imprinted
on its crystalline page.

Flower of the sky, flower of the water,
the soul of the lake is a swan
with two human pupils,
serious and genteel as a prince;
iris wings, rose legs . . .
Burning beak, sad neck
and proud, and the whiteness
and the softness of a swan . . .

The candid and serious bird
has a wicked charm;
—carnation dressed in iris,
he transcends flame and miracle . . . !
His white wings move me
like two hot arms;
no lips have burned
as his beak in my hands;
no head has fallen
as listless on my lap;

ninguna carne tan viva,
he padecido o gozado:
Viborean en sus venas
filtros dos veces humanos!

Del rubí de la lujuria
su testa está coronada;
y va arrastrando el deseo
en una cauda rosada . . .

Agua le doy en mis manos
y él parece beber fuego;
y yo parezco ofrecerle
todo el vaso de mi cuerpo . . .

Y vive tanto en mis sueños,
y ahonda tanto en mi carne,
que a veces pienso si el cisne
con sus dos alas fugaces,
sus raros ojos humanos
y el rojo pico quemante,
es sólo un cisne en mi lago
o es en mi vida un amante . . .

Al margen del lago claro
yo le interrogo en silencio . . .
y el silencio es una rosa
sobre su pico de fuego . . .

no flesh so alive
have I suffered or enjoyed:
Philters twice those of a human
snake through his veins!

His head crowned
by a ruby of lust,
as he trails pink desire
from the train of a bishop's robe . . .

Water I give him from my hands
but it seems he drinks fire;
and it seems I offer him
the entire cup of my body . . .

And he lives so in my dreams,
and he delves so deep in my flesh,
that at times I wonder if the swan
with his two evanescent wings,
his strange human eyes
and burning red beak,
is but a swan on my lake
or in my life a lover . . .

On the edge of the clear lake
I interrogate him in silence . . .
And the silence is a rose
on his beak of fire . . .

Pero en su carne me habla
y yo en mi carne le entiendo.
—A veces ¡toda! soy alma;
y a veces ¡toda! soy cuerpo.—
Hunde el pico en mi regazo
y se queda como muerto . . .
Y en la cristalina página,
en el sensitivo espejo
del lago que algunas veces
refleja mi pensamiento,
el cisne asusta de rojo,
y yo de blanca doy miedo!

But his flesh speaks to me
and in my flesh I understand him.
—At times I am—entirely!—soul;
at times I am—entirely!—body.—
He sinks his beak into my lap
and is later as if dead . . .
And on the crystalline page,
on the sensitive looking glass
of the lake that at times
reflects my thoughts,
the swan's red frightens,
and I'm so white that I scare!

(trans. SW)

Nocturno

Engarzado en la noche el lago de tu alma,
diríase una tela de cristal y de calma
tramada por las grandes arañas del desvelo.

Nata de agua lustral en vaso de alabastros;
espejo de pureza que abrillantas los astros
y reflejas la cima de la Vida en un cielo! . . .

Y soy el cisne errante de los sangrientos rastros,
voy manchando los lagos y remontando el vuelo.

Nocturne

The lake of your soul mounted in a setting of night,
like a woven-cloth web of calm and crystal
spun by the giant spiders of sleeplessness.

Sheen of lustral water in an alabaster vessel;
purity's mirror, you make the stars shine brighter
and you reflect in a heaven the depths of Life! . . .

And I am the wandering swan of the bloodstained wake,
I taint lake upon lake and off I soar.

Works Cited in the Headnotes and Footnotes

Agustini, Delmira. *Poesías completas*. Ed. Alejandro Cáceres. Montevideo: Plaza, 1999.

Armas, Emilio de. *Casal*. Havana: Letras Cubanas, 1981.

Augier, Ángel I. *Juana Borrero, la adolescente atormentada*. Havana: Molina, 1938.

Baudelaire, Charles, "Spleen(2)." *The Flowers of Evil*. Bilingual ed. Trans. James McGowan. Oxford World's Classics. Oxford: Oxford UP, 1993. 146–47.

Bécquer, Gustavo Adolfo. "Rima VII." *Rimas*. Centro Virtual Cervantes. 2002–06. 13 Oct. 2006 <http://cvc.cervantes.es/obref/rimas/rimas/rima13.htm>.

Borges, Jorge Luis, and Betina Edelberg. "Leopoldo Lugones." *Obras completas en colaboración*. Buenos Aires: Emecé, 1979. 461–62.

Brotherston, Gordon, ed. *Spanish American Modernista Poets: A Critical Anthology*. 2nd ed. London: Bristol Classical; Newburyport: Focus Information Group, 1995.

Casal, Julián del. *Poesías completas y pequeños poemas en prosa en orden cronológico*. Ed. Esperanza Figueroa. Miami: Universal, 1993.

Darío, Rubén. "Dilucidaciones." *Páginas escogidas*. Ed. Ricardo Gullón. Madrid: Cátedra, 1991. 125–37.

Díaz Mirón, Salvador. *Poesía completa*. Ed. Manuel Sol. Mexico City: Fondo de Cultura Económica, 1997.

Eguren, José Mariá. "Las bodas vienesas." *Poemas de José María Eguren*. Ed. Justo Alarcón. 7 Sept. 2002. 19 Oct. 2006 <http://www.los-poetas.com/c/engur1.htm>.

Gautier, Théophile. "Symphonie en blanc majeur." *The Oxford Book of French Verse*. 1920. Comp. St. John Lucas. Bartleby. com. 2005. 13 Oct. 2006 <http://www.bartleby.net/244/282.html>.

Gutiérrez Nájera, Manuel. "El arte y el materialismo." 1876. *Obras: Crítica literaria*. Vol. 1. Mexico: U Nacional Autónoma de México, 1959. 49–64.

Herrera y Reissig, Julio. *Poesías completas y páginas en prosa*. Ed. Roberto Bula Piriz. Madrid: Aguilar, 1961.

Horace. *The Complete Odes and Epodes*. Trans. David West. Oxford World's Classics. Oxford: Oxford UP, 2000.

"Hou'ri." *Brewer's Dictionary of Phrase and Fable*. 1898. Bartleby.com. 2000. 20 Oct. 2006 <http://www.bartleby.com/81/8533.html>.

Jaimes Freyre, Ricardo. "Los antepasados." Freyre, *Poemas*.

———. "El camino de los cisnes." Freyre, *Poemas*.

———. *Poemas de Ricardo Jaimes Freyre*. Ed. Justo S. Alarcón. 15 May 2000. 16 Oct. 2006 <http://www.los-poetas.com/f/frey1.htm>.

Jiménez, José Olivio, ed. *Antología crítica del modernismo*. Madrid: Hiperión, 1994.

Jrade, Cathy Login. *Modernismo, Modernity, and the Development of Spanish American Literature*. Austin: U of Texas P, 1998.

Lugones, Leopoldo. "Jaculatoria lunar." *Lunario sentimental*. Ed. Jesús Benítez. Madrid: Cátedra, 1988. 136–37.

———. "Prólogo." *Castalia bárbara y otros poemas*. By Ricardo Jaimes Freyre. Mexico City: Cultura, 1920. x–xxi.

Martí, José. *Poesía completa*. Ed. Carlos Javier Morales. Madrid: Alianza, 1995.

McIntosh, Christopher. *The Swan King*. New York: Palgrave-Macmillan, 2003.

Monner Sans, José María. "Juana Borrero." *Julián del Casal y el modernismo hispanoamericano*. Mexico City: El Colegio de México, 1952. 250–54.

Moréas, Jean. "Le symbolisme." *Figaro* 18 Sept. 1886, literary supplement: 1–2. 12 Oct. 2006 <http://www.berlol.net/chrono/chr1886a.htm>.

Neruda, Pablo. *Canto General*. Trans. Jack Schmitt. Berkeley: U of California P, 2000.

Paz, Octavio, ed. *Mexican Poetry: An Anthology*. Trans. Samuel Beckett. Bloomington: Indiana UP, 1958.

Petronius. *The Satyricon*. Trans. and introd. Alfred R. Allinson. New York: Panurge, 1930. Internet Sacred Texts Archive. 2006. 17 Oct. 2006 <http://www.sacred-texts.com/cla/petro/satyr/index.htm>.

Poe, Edgar Allan. "Ulalume." *American Review* Dec. 1847: 599–600. *The Works of Edgar Allan Poe*. Edgar Allan Poe Soc. of Baltimore. 29 Aug. 1998. 16 Oct. 2006 <http://www.lfchosting.com/eapoe/works/poems/ulalumea.htm>.

Rosenbaum, Sidonia Carmen. *Modern Women Poets of Spanish America*. New ed. Westport: Greenwood, 1978.

Santos Chocano, José. *Obras completas*. Ed. Luis Alberto Sánchez. Mexico City: Aguilar, 1954.

Seeger, Alan. *Poems by Alan Seeger*. Project Gutenberg. 23 Sept. 2006. 16 Oct. 2006 <http://www.gutenberg.org/etext/617>.

Silva, José Asunción. *De sobremesa.* Madrid: Hiperión, 1996. Trans. as *After-Dinner Conversation: The Diary of a Decadent.* Trans. Kelly Washbourne. Austin: U of Texas P, 2005.

———. "Estrellas que entre lo sombrío. . . ." *Poemas de José Asunción Silva.* Los-poetas.com. 7 Sept. 2002. 13 Oct. 2006 <http://www.los-poetas.com/b/silva2.htm#INDICE>.

Valdés, María Elena de. "Women Writing in Nontraditional Genres." *Literary Cultures of Latin America: A Comparative History.* Ed. Mario J. Valdés and Djelal Kadir. Vol. 1. Oxford: Oxford UP, 2004. 315–27.

Valencia, Guillermo. "Leyendo a Silva." Brotherston 110–16.

"Veneficial." *The Oxford English Dictionary.* 2nd ed. 1989.

Verlaine, Paul. "Art poétique." *One Hundred and One Poems by Paul Verlaine.* Bilingual ed. Trans. Norman R. Shapiro. Chicago: U of Chicago P, 1999. 126–28.

———. "Crimen Amoris." *Selected Poems.* Ed. and trans. Clark Ashton Smith. Sauk City: Arkham, 1971. 223–26.

Visconti, Luchino, dir. *Ludwig.* Mega, Cinetel, Dieter Geissler Filmproduktions, and Divina, 1972.

Yeats, William Butler. "Leda and the Swan." *The Collected Poems of W. B. Yeats.* 2nd ed. Ed. Richard J. Finneran. New York: Scribner's, 1996. 214.

Zárate, Armando. *Literatura hispanoamericana de protesta social: Una poética de la libertad.* Lanham: UP of Amer., 1994.

Modern Language Association of America Texts and Translations

Texts

Anna Banti. *"La signorina" e altri racconti.* Ed. and introd. Carol Lazzaro-Weis. 2001.

Adolphe Belot. *Mademoiselle Giraud, ma femme.* Ed and introd. Christopher Rivers. 2002.

Dovid Bergelson. אָפּגאַנג. Ed. and introd. Joseph Sherman. 1999.

Elsa Bernstein. *Dämmerung: Schauspiel in fünf Akten.* Ed. and introd. Susanne Kord. 2003.

Edith Bruck. *Lettera alla madre.* Ed. and introd. Gabriella Romani. 2006.

Isabelle de Charrière. *Lettres de Mistriss Henley publiées par son amie.* Ed. Joan Hinde Stewart and Philip Stewart. 1993.

Isabelle de Charrière. *Trois femmes: Nouvelle de l'Abbe de la Tour.* Ed. and introd. Emma Rooksby. 2007.

François-Timoléon de Choisy, Marie-Jeanne L'Héritier, and Charles Perrault. *Histoire de la Marquise-Marquis de Banneville.* Ed. Joan DeJean. 2004.

Sophie Cottin. *Claire d'Albe.* Ed. and introd. Margaret Cohen. 2002.

Claire de Duras. *Ourika.* Ed. Joan DeJean. Introd. Joan DeJean and Margaret Waller. 1994.

Şeyh Galip. *Hüsn ü Aşk.* Ed. and introd. Victoria Rowe Holbrook. 2005.

Françoise de Graffigny. *Lettres d'une Péruvienne.* Introd. Joan DeJean and Nancy K. Miller. 1993.

Sofya Kovalevskaya. Нигилистка. Ed. and introd. Natasha Kolchevska. 2001.

Thérèse Kuoh-Moukoury. *Rencontres essentielles.* Introd. Cheryl Toman. 2002.

Juan José Millás. *"Trastornos de carácter" y otros cuentos.* Introd. Pepa Anastasio. 2007.

Emilia Pardo Bazán. *"El encaje roto" y otros cuentos.* Ed. and introd. Joyce Tolliver. 1996.

Rachilde. *Monsieur Vénus: Roman matérialiste.* Ed. and introd. Melanie Hawthorne and Liz Constable. 2004.

Marie Riccoboni. *Histoire d'Ernestine.* Ed. Joan Hinde Stewart and Philip Stewart. 1998.

Eleonore Thon. *Adelheit von Rastenberg.* Ed. and introd. Karin A. Wurst. 1996.

Translations

Anna Banti. *"The Signorina" and Other Stories.* Trans. Martha King and Carol Lazzaro-Weis. 2001.

Adolphe Belot. *Mademoiselle Giraud, My Wife.* Trans. Christopher Rivers. 2002.

Dovid Bergelson. *Descent.* Trans. Joseph Sherman. 1999.

Elsa Bernstein. *Twilight: A Drama in Five Acts.* Trans. Susanne Kord. 2003.

Edith Bruck. *Letter to My Mother.* Trans. Brenda Webster with Gabriella Romani. 2006.

Isabelle de Charrière. *Letters of Mistress Henley Published by Her Friend.* Trans. Philip Stewart and Jean Vaché. 1993.

Isabelle de Charrière. *Three Women: A Novel by the Abbé de la Tour.* Trans. Emma Rooksby. 2007.

François-Timoléon de Choisy, Marie-Jeanne L'Héritier, and Charles Perrault. *The Story of the Marquise-Marquis de Banneville.* Trans. Steven Rendall. 2004.

Sophie Cottin. *Claire d'Albe.* Trans. Margaret Cohen. 2002.

Claire de Duras. *Ourika.* Trans. John Fowles. 1994.

Şeyh Galip. *Beauty and Love.* Trans. Victoria Rowe Holbrook. 2005.

Françoise de Graffigny. *Letters from a Peruvian Woman.* Trans. David Kornacker. 1993.

Sofya Kovalevskaya. *Nihilist Girl.* Trans. Natasha Kolchevska with Mary Zirin. 2001.

Thérèse Kuoh-Moukoury. *Essential Encounters.* Trans. Cheryl Toman. 2002.

Juan José Millás. *"Personality Disorders" and Other Stories.* Trans. Gregory B. Kaplan. 2007.

Emilia Pardo Bazán. *"Torn Lace" and Other Stories.* Trans. María Cristina Urruela. 1996.

Rachilde. *Monsieur Vénus: A Materialist Novel.* Trans. Melanie Hawthorne. 2004.

Marie Riccoboni. *The Story of Ernestine.* Trans. Joan Hinde Stewart and Philip Stewart. 1998.

Eleonore Thon. *Adelheit von Rastenberg.* Trans. George F. Peters. 1996.

Texts and Translations in One Volume

جدید اردو شاعری کا انتخاب / *An Anthology of Modern Urdu Poetry.* Ed., introd., and trans. M. A. R. Habib. 2003.

An Anthology of Spanish American Modernismo. Ed. Kelly Washbourne. Trans. Kelly Washbourne with Sergio Waisman. 2007.